CW01509002

Cover Design: Graeme Clarke
graeme@graemeclarke.co.uk

Typesetting by Fledgling Press Ltd
www.fledglingpress.co.uk

Books by Linda Tweedie & Kate McGregor

Life Behind Bars: Confessions of a Pub Landlady

Life on the Outside

Foreword

Life in the Fat Lane is based loosely on the experiences of the Authors, both being fat buggers. The ladies have battled constantly throughout their adult lives with weight issues and have consistently LOST!

So in this era of low-fat //no fat//gluten -free//cooking - the Atkins diet – the Zone Diet – the – Less than Ten Calories a Day diet, we meet a small group of panic -dieters, who at one time or another have tried them all, and who, for whatever reason, must lose weight NOW. In most cases, an extraordinary huge amount of weight in a very limited time, so anything goes.

Their lives are governed by what they can eat and what they can't. Yet no matter how good or bad each individual has been, most dieters stay the same or worse, get worse!

Join them on their hysterical and sometimes poignant journey to thinness. Meet Selena, who is desperate to become a mother, Kylie, a spoiled, deluded, selfish young woman who knows it all. Julie, the diet guru, is simply as mad as a hatter and finally Cheryl who just wants to meet her Prince Charming and live happily ever after – fat chance.

LIFE IN THE FAT LANE

KYLIE

I only eat three times a day -- morning, noon, and night.

What a shit of a day, mused Kylie as she licked the remains of the chocolate wrapper, straining to reach every last morsel. She hated Mondays. In fact, she hated Tuesdays, Wednesdays and Thursdays. Fridays were okay only because she finished work at noon. Hey! Who was she kidding? She hated Fridays too. In fact she hated her job, but she'd hated every job she'd ever had, and boy had she had some.

Today had been worse than usual. Bill the foreman had been on her case since she'd clocked on. Okay, so she was a bit late – half an hour or so. (If truth be told it was closer to an hour). C'mon it was Monday and everyone was late on a Monday. But for God's sake he had gone on and on, never letting up. In fact, he had picked on her all day. He wasn't too pleased either when she asked to go on an early lunch.

So what if she'd only been at her bench for forty minutes? What she could do in forty minutes was more than all those smarmy buggers who came in on time put together. Well, except Andrew and maybe Poofy Pete, and of course Margaret was fast, my God was she fast. Gladys wasn't too slow either. Well, so what, she was as good as any of them, well as good as most of them. Whatever! What did it matter, there was no way she was going to stay for another ten years just so she could gut a fish in thirty seconds. No chance! She was destined for greater things. She wasn't sure what, but better than spending her life with her hand up a fish's arse.

To make matters worse, lunch had been a disaster. She was desperate to catch up with Jason, her boyfriend of two weeks, but he and Mandy, her BFF since nursery days, were on the missing list. She had endured a rollicking from Bill, only to find that Mandy had thrown the old chestnut, 'The Dentist' and was off into town with Jason. Her Jason! Wasn't she supposed to be the one going out with Jason? So what the hell was Mandy playing at?

Neither of them had answered her calls or texts for hours and when they eventually got round to remembering she was alive, they had given her some cock-and-bull rubbish about having no signal. As if. And to top it all Mandy had the cheek to be miffed at the twenty nine missed calls, yelling in front of everyone that she was a bunny boiler and a deluded psycho. What the hell had rabbits to do with anything? And deluded? She didn't want either of them to know she had no idea what deluded meant. Then it had dawned on her, not the deluded thingy. Of course, her birthday, that's what all the secrecy had been about. They had been into town to buy her birthday present and she had nearly spoiled the surprise, no wonder they were annoyed. Never mind, she'd make it up to them both at the weekend, she could do surprises too.

Lost in her fluffy daydream of puppies and kittens with pink ribbons and enormous boxes of chocolates, she almost passed out with fright. Bawling in her ear was bloody Bill. What was he going on about now? How dare he say she was holding up production? Her? He was having a laugh. She might report him to management, it would serve him right. Every time she looked up, there he was staring. Wherever she went, he popped up. She couldn't sneak as much as a quick puff without him bearing down on her and droning on about quotas and workloads. She got the feeling he had sussed her out about the smoking though, well, it wasn't fair. Non-smokers had to work straight through, whereas smokers got a five minute break every hour. So she had just let them think she smoked. She wasn't the only one. Well, she suspected she was, but so what? It was sexual harassment, or victimization, or something.

If she as much as looked at her phone he was down on her like a ton of bricks. Okay, she knew she wasn't supposed to use her mobile during working hours but it had been an emergency. It had! She hadn't been able to contact the two most important people in her world, so it was an emergency. Well, maybe not exactly, but it was causing her undue stress which of course affected her production.

She decided she'd better get her head down for the

rest of the day and keep out of his line of fire. She had a fair bit of work to catch up on, and for some reason none of her so-called workmates seemed inclined to help her out.

"Well, screw them," she muttered as she flounced back to her work station, barging past Poofy Pete, sending him crashing into a box of live crabs and causing him to almost dismember himself.

Pete was squealing like a boiled lobster and there was blood everywhere and crabs on the loose. Christ, she'd had bigger paper cuts. She was in for it big time. Bill looked like he was about to have a heart attack.

She could feel the laughter rising up through her belly and about to explode out of her mouth. She daren't. OMG she really daren't. He would bloody murder her, not sack her.

She had to divert his attention, nothing else for it. She threw herself down on the ground and made out she was having a fit. But it was nothing compared to the one her boss was having.

It was like a scene from a pantomime. Poofy Pete, never one to miss a drama, was demanding medical attention. Then there was a seventeen stone lump of a girl faking an epileptic fit (badly). Dozens of crabs making a bid for freedom (and those buggers could shift). The rest of the posse were standing around looking even more bewildered than usual.

All Kylie could think of as she was thrashing about amidst fish guts, blood and scales, was that no-one would sit beside her on the way home tonight and she was right. Mind you, she was seldom bothered by companions on the journey home. Her girth was such that she left room for only the teeniest of passengers, but even they would be sure to avoid this rank-smelling lump.

Not one person came to her assistance; all they were concerned about was Pete. He had been given sweet tea, chocolate digestive biscuits and was wearing some kind of dead cat round his neck to keep him warm. Apparently he was in shock, someone commented. In shock? He'd be fucking traumatised for life if he saw himself in that mangy, flea-ridden old thing. But all that was by-the-by. What attention had she had? Sweet tea? Nope! Digestive biscuits, plain or chocolate? Nope. Any old blanket or tarpaulin to keep her warm? Nope.

"Charming, absolutely fucking charming," she thought. "Hey I'm having a fit here, is no one interested? I could have choked on my tongue, you lot."

"That would be highly unlikely," sneered Gladys. "It's always too far up your own arse."

"Is no-one going to get me a cup of tea?" she pleaded.

There was no answer. In fact, by now most of the work-force had drifted back to their stations, the drama over, as Pete had been carted off to the Medical Room. She realised no-one was paying any attention to her flailing about like a beached whale.

"Would someone kindly help me up?" She snarled, again no response.

"I said would someone kindly help me up?" Everyone seemed very preoccupied with the intestines of the particular poisson they were handling and she, with as much dignity as a seventeen stone lass can muster, crawled over to her table and hoisted herself up.

"Thanks a bunch," she muttered.

"Well, no-one here wants to put their back out heaving your huge carcase up," smirked Bill.

"Cheeky sod," she said dumbstruck.

What was he trying to say? That she was fat? Fucking cheek. Okay, she wasn't a size ten, but on a good day she could squeeze into a respectable sixteen. She had big bones. Everyone knew she had big bones. All her family suffered from big bones. In fact she was the petite one. Fucking fat, she'd give him fat, the ugly bastard!

How she got through the remainder of the day she did not know. That little creep Pete was whinging on and on about his finger. He was sure he probably needed stitches so he went running off to have a rest. He felt faint and all those funny buggers in packing were making stupid jokes about whales and crabs and having fits. The only relief was that Bill had disappeared off to Human Resources and she didn't see him for the rest of the day.

He was probably worried she'd put in a claim for

inadequate first aid facilities. After all, no-one had seemed to know what to do when she was having her fit. Maybe she could get a few quid out of this? The fact that she had been faking it had completely slipped her mind.

Cheryl

Obesity is a growing problem.

OMG, OMG, was it true? Was it really, really true? Had it actually happened? Hugging herself. Please don't let it have been a dream or worse still, some kind of sick joke. She couldn't bear it if it wasn't true.

Last night had been the best night of her life. She was ecstatic, absolutely over the moon. Why? He had actually proposed to her. The love of her life had, unbelievably, gone down on one knee and asked her to marry him. She could hardly believe it, but there was the proof – a fabulous, magnificent ring, glinting on her left hand. Shame it was on the wrong finger but that could be easily sorted. Just like the others.

Doug was such a generous guy, always buying her gifts, but Cheryl nearly always had to have them re-sized without him knowing. It was obvious most of the women he knew were a size 0 or smaller. But this, my God, this was a proper engagement ring. A beautiful, magnificent, proper ring, she kept repeating to herself. She had never thought she'd ever receive such a token. But squealing with joy and dancing around the room, she had.

Wait till she told them at work, that would show them; all those smartasses, the doubters, the ones who didn't believe Doug even existed. She knew the word at the water cooler was that she had just made up this fabulous boyfriend. Nobody had seen him, nobody had taken a call from him, so what? She was a private person. She didn't broadcast every detail of her life to all and sundry, didn't boast about what Doug had bought her or when he'd sent flowers. On the one occasion he'd sent a magnificent bouquet to work, it was the general consensus that she'd sent them to herself. Why would no-one believe her? Why couldn't she receive flowers on her birthday or Valentine's Day without the world judging her?

Cheryl had been introduced to Doug by one of her many friends, she couldn't remember off-hand which one, she had so many. And fortunately they had hit it off immediately. It was amazing, they had the same taste in music, in movies, books and food. They were both real foodies and spent hours extolling the virtues of different spices and herbs. If he liked something, chances were she would and vice versa. It really seemed impossible that two people could be so alike. In fact they were so perfectly matched they would joke that a computer couldn't have paired them any better. But marriage, whoa, that was something else.

Like many couples who find love, they had been friends for quite some time before moving up a gear. They knew almost everything about each other and over the months had found their feelings towards one another had changed. It became apparent that not only were they best friends, but they had fallen in love, they were true soulmates.

They spent almost all their free time together, maybe to the detriment of other friendships, but they both agreed that for the moment they didn't need anyone else. Each more than fulfilled the needs of the other, so apart from sleeping, working and eating, their lives were inseparable.

Only one snag, they had never actually met!

In the beginning, just like twenty million other people, Cheryl had posted her profile online and on the pretext of wishing anonymity, had declined to show any photographs.

It had been years since she had subjected herself to having her photograph taken. The last time had probably been her cousin's wedding, aged twelve and wearing an enormous pink meringue of a dress. She had looked like a huge marshmallow and since then, had avoided the camera like the plague. In the ensuing years, any snapshots she had taken were usually for some official reason: driving licence or travel pass, and all less than complimentary.

She was okay for head shots, mainly due to her crowning glory – her magnificent titian mane. It was, without a doubt, her best feature. With her dark green eyes and clear fair skin she had a look of the Celt about her. She was, in fact, a very striking woman, and with just a little effort would look stunning. But that was not her problem; Cheryl was a big girl, a very big girl. But she was also a big girl who was a wizard with Photoshop.

Seeing Doug's profile, she knew in her heart that no matter how alike they were and how many interests they shared, it was most unlikely that he would fall for the real Cheryl. She so loved him and couldn't imagine her life without him in it.

Her first deception had just been a little cheat. There was nothing she couldn't do with images so she had just altered hers a little, only a little. What had she done? Well, she was reasonably satisfied with her well-airbrushed head shot, but the body? He would run a mile. He would definitely unfriend her, cut her off, and she couldn't have that, so she had simply grafted her head shot on to a more attractive body.

Why not? And she had to say the "new" her was just fabulous. She was swamped with requests from other friends, but she wasn't interested. Doug was "The One" and Kim Kardashian's butt had never looked better.

For the first time ever Cheryl was sexy, real eye candy. A showstopper and it seemed the woman of Doug's dreams. The woman Doug had proposed to. Also the woman Doug proposed coming to visit in under three months. Shit, what was she going to do? She had to lose five stones in three months.

Call it fate or karma, but just at that precise moment a flyer fell out of the morning paper. FAT FIGHTERS 4 YOU. And they had a class starting at 6pm, just round the corner. She'd go, give it a try while she still had the courage. Even though she still suffered nightmares over the last class she had attended.

Cheryl did not possess a set of scales. They wouldn't have done her much good anyway, they probably didn't go up high enough. Nor did she have a full length mirror, so it had been years since she knew what she weighed or what she looked like. You can imagine the traumatic experience she had had on her first visit to a slimming club, with a couple of the girls from the office, when things went dreadfully wrong.

As Cheryl nervously joined the line of members to be weighed she caught sight of a familiar face. Couldn't think who it was, but my God, what a weight she'd put on. How could anyone let themselves get to that size? It was ridiculous, almost obscene.

As she reached her turn she was sure the scales screamed out loud when registering her bulk. But no, it wasn't the scales screaming, it was her. The big fat horror that had looked familiar was her, and the class counsellor was so flustered by Cheryl's reaction she blurted out her weight for everyone to hear.

She had left the class in tears, vowing never to return, but forgetting about the other slimmers, many of whom were known to her. A few were sympathetic to her plight, but come on, we all love a bit of gossip. They had relayed the whole sorry episode at the water cooler the following morning. Poor Cheryl, she was subjected to a barrage of jokes and screams for many months to follow. She had seldom participated in any work outings before this incident. They were a complete no-no from then on.

But here she was, willing to give it another try. She'd go on her own and tell no-one. So at 6pm that evening there she was, outside the church hall, emblazoned with Fat Fighter 4 You posters willing her to join. Standing amidst a dozen or so little Brownies, waiting for their mums to collect them, all having quite a hilarious time at the expense of the very large lady who was debating whether or not to venture forth into the almost unknown. Her courage failed her and just as she was about to turn back and re-trace her footsteps the worst thing imaginable happened.

Julie happened. Julie from the post room happened, the absolute worst encounter possible.

"Hello, love, didn't know you were a member here. Good, I'll have someone to sit beside during class. Hey, it must be good, you look like you've lost a bit of weight..." she prattled on.

"Only because I've probably shit myself seeing you here," Cheryl murmured to herself.

"New members over here for registration," a very officious person called out to them.

"Oh, you're new too!" enthused Julie. "Great, we can be diet buddies. Brilliant."

"Yes, brilliant," muttered a very downhearted Cheryl. If she reads out my weight so help me I'll deck her, she thought, glaring at the counsellor.

Lord above, as if it could get any worse. She'd recognise that booming laugh anywhere. Selena. Loud, brash, and as for discreet? Cheryl would be as well announcing her situation on the giant billboard outside. Selena from accounts was beckoning her and Julie to come and sit beside her. Shit!

Kylie

Milk chocolate is a dairy product.

The bus was packed with workers on their way home, but her earlier thoughts had proved right. She had the whole seat to herself. No-one seemed inclined to share with her, one of the few perks of working in a fish factory. That, and the fact she took up most of the remaining space (although she would never admit that). Kylie had been lost in a very pleasant daydream. She was getting a huge pay-off from the Industrial Injuries Tribunal and Bill was being sacked for mismanagement and she was being offered his job, when suddenly, the bus jolted violently and dammit, she dropped the remainder of her second Mars bar.

Jesus suffering, could today get any worse?

Cursing the incompetent driver and the inconsiderate fool who had been stupid enough to throw himself under her bus, she scrambled about on the floor looking for her missing bar amongst her discarded sandwich wrappers, toffee papers, and a couple of empty cans. Well, it was a long journey and she'd missed most of lunch. No luck, there wasn't any sign of her precious Mars bar. She furiously scanned the other passengers to see if some thieving beggar had found it and was enjoying their ill-gotten gains, but no, they all seemed more interested in what was going on outside.

Heavens, she hoped she wasn't going to be late for tea, she was bloody famished.

Peering out of the window, and hoping against hope that the bus would soon continue on its journey, she was hit by another jolt. What was that? Had someone smacked her? Was she faint due to lack of sustenance? Had the driver hit someone else? Lord, she hoped not. Shit, tea would be definitely over if that was the case. In her house it was not a case of first come, first served, it was more first come, none left. She'd have to queue for ages in the chippie.

Then she saw it, the most amazing, fabulous, stunningly beautiful dress she had ever seen. She couldn't take her eyes off it, the Mars bar completely forgotten. There in all its glory, in the window of Madam Jessica's, was the dress of her dreams. This would certainly make Jason swoon and Mandy green with envy. But Madam Jessica's was the most exclusive and expensive shop in town. She had never looked inside its auspicious portals, let alone entered them.

Before she knew it, she was on her feet and heading towards this mirage. Down the stairs and off the stationary bus. Oops, she seemed to have stepped on something.

What the devil was everyone shouting about? Okay, okay, she hadn't seen the man lying stretched out, bloody stupid place to lie down anyway. What was the problem? He'd already been hit by a bus, so what more damage could little old she do?

Looking down at her once-white work clothes and boots, she wasn't exactly dressed for a visit to Madam Jessica's. In fact, she'd never be exactly dressed for a visit there. Removing a dead fish eye from her pocket, she peered through the window and came face to face with the terrifying gaze of Madam Jessica. She almost about-turned but no, the dress had to be hers.

The door opened and the dragon lady seemed to be beckoning her in. She was holding out the precious dress as if she knew it was meant for Kylie.

"Goodness what on earth is going on outside? Has there been some kind of accident?"

Watching the commotion,, Madam Jessica was intrigued by the antics of those concerned; the bus driver, the cyclist, (who was obviously an ambulance chaser) and the various onlookers. Presumably someone had called for help, not that she would be getting involved. Maison Jessica was far too elite an establishment to be embroiled in a mélange with a bus and a bike. A Rolls Royce and a Daimler maybe, but a bus and a bike? No.

She could see that the cyclist had sustained no life-threatening injuries but was making a real drama out of it. This was definitely a No Win – No Fee job and he was milking it for all it was worth. He was laid out on the pavement with a tatty old blanket over him and a small blonde woman holding his hand, perhaps checking to make sure he still had a pulse, amidst an increasingly curious crowd.

Oh, goodness, the poor man. A huge girl had just stepped from the bus, not seeming to notice the cyclist and all twenty stone of her strode purposefully across the poor man's chest. The cyclist seemed to have taken a dramatic turn for the worse and the passengers and driver were scurrying about.

Dear God in heaven. She jumped as she caught sight of a massive round face pressed to the glass. Good Lord, she thought, bloody care in the community.

She couldn't have faces like that pressed against her glass, that wouldn't do. Opening the door to shoo the creature away, she was almost flattened as the large person from the bus barged into the shop.

Was this a ram raid? She was certainly built for it. Despite her posh accent and Parisienne couture, Madam Jessica had grown up in the East End as plain, streetwise Jessie Grey. Nor had she survived the catfights on the catwalks without learning a trick or two. She could certainly hold her own in most situations, but this was a BIG girl. However, if need be there was a host of uniformed men not twenty yards from where she stood.

"Ken aye help you?" In her poshest accent she addressed the huge person.

"The dress, the dress that was in the window," stammered Kylie. "It hasn't been sold has it?"

Holding on to the precious gown, Madam Jessica looked at this monster, which incidentally smelled appalling.

"This gown? Are you enquairing about this gown?"

"Yeah, yeah, that one," answered the troll.

"May dear, this 'ere gown is an original Reephoff. Comprendez? It is a one-off."

"Uh huh, but is it for sale?" asked Kylie, even more enthralled.

"Did you understand me, dearie? This is an exclusive designer gown and costs almost a thousand pounds."

"Yeah, yeah whatever. But is it still for sale and what size is it?" the troll demanded.

"It is £999 and it's a model size twelve, with a generous seam allowance," replied Madam Jessica.

Completely overawed by the shop, the dragon lady and the dress, Kylie was having difficulty breathing. She couldn't follow what the dragon lady was saying; all she could make out was Rip Off. The woman seemed to think she was there to mug her off.

Was the dress still for sale? How could she get through to this dragon with the foreign accent? She certainly didn't come from round here. She had to have it. Was there some other customer lurking in the dark recesses of the shop, waiting to try on her dress?

Kylie had to have it. Mind you, a grand was a lot to pay for one night. But hey, Ma and the boys would stump up for her happiness and it could be a birthday present.

She could just see herself dancing with Jason at the party and everyone looking on jealously.

She knew that to fulfil her dream she couldn't eat for the next six weeks. Well, with what she would save on Mars bars and Snickers, she could easily pay for the dress herself.

Speaking very slowly so that the dragon lady would understand, she asked what size it was. Unable to decipher the reply, she assumed it to be about a size twelve. Maybe they had one in a bigger size? No? It seemed to be the only one, the words exclusive and a one-off featured prominently in the answer. Bugger, it had to be a diet then.

Still speaking in words of one syllable, Kylie told Madam Jessica she would have the dress, but she would have to put a deposit down as she didn't have enough money with her today. But she had to have the dress and she would pay the balance on Friday.

The woman seemed to be having some kind of attack. Jesus, had she not had enough of those today without this old biddy freaking out on her?

Bewildered, Kylie realised the woman was laughing. Laughing at her? Why? Stupid old fool, she thought as she left the shop.

JULIE

If weight is a number, then mine is unlisted.

Mm, this is a new one, mused Julie, picking up a leaflet that someone had dropped. FAT FIGHTERS 4 YOU was emblazoned along the top of the leaflet. Very interesting, very scientific, she thought. She liked scientific. Scientific and celebrity, they were the key diets to follow, according to Julie. Not seen this one before, she thought, and by heavens, there weren't many diets Julie had not seen.

Might give this a try, she twittered to herself. Classes start at 6pm on Wednesday nights. That's tonight. It might be a bit of a squeeze but... Maybe she could fit it in between her 5pm Slimming Success and 7.30 Big Losers. And the first class is free, better still. Yep, she told herself, she would pop along and see what they had to offer.

She could do with a new slant, she convinced herself. She'd kind of plateaued over the past couple of months. Stayed the same – neither up nor down – and it was depressing, to say the least. For someone who was a serial dieter, in fact, she was a diaddict. How could she not be losing weight? Let's face it, she spent enough time and money on weight control.

She attended Slimming World and Pilates on Mondays; Diet Divas on Tuesdays (had to get home sharp for the boys); Slim Success and Big Losers on Wednesday. Thursday was Aqua Aerobics and Kick Boxing and Friday was Hypnotherapy and Aversion Therapy, two for the price of one. So this new one might just do the trick and kickstart her back on track.

She had pink pills, blue pills, green and yellow capsules, Go Jo Berries by the crate load; creams, lotions and dozens of potions. Cream to rub on, cream to rub off and cream to swallow (well, that was a bit of a faux pas, lost in the Spanish translation!). Mind you, it had worked for a while, but had tasted awful.

As for diets, well, there was the Atkins, Hollywood, Mayo Clinic, Californian Beach Diet, Calorie Counting Cabbage Diet (hated that one!) and 5:2. She'd been doing that before anyone had even heard of it. Gee-whiz she could have made a fortune if she'd thought to put it down on paper. The Banana Diet, Macrobiotic Diet, Animal Diet (she never wanted to be reminded of that one!) and as for Slimming Clubs, she was a lifetime member of almost every one.

Once upon a time, Julie had been a normal everyday young woman. She was reasonably attractive, wouldn't win Miss World but had no shortage of admirers. A happy-go lucky popular girl until she met Bobby.

They were introduced at the tennis club and Julie was smitten at once. Lightning bolt, love at first sight. He was so good-looking and oh, how he smelled. Bobby had just qualified as an accountant when they first met. He was very ambitious, hardworking and she absolutely adored him. Although from time to time she sometime got that niggling feeling that maybe their relationship was a bit one-sided, but she had no real doubts.

It had been a traditional white wedding; four bridesmaids and a flower girl, held in the town's best hotel and Julie knew on that special day she had looked every bit as beautiful as any bride, or for that matter, any film star. Life was wonderful.

It wasn't long before the babies came along. Twins who were a handful from the start. Julie had had her work cut out keeping the house, the babies and herself up to Bobby's exacting standards. It was hard going, but Julie loved her life and felt privileged to have it.

She was happiest when the house was shining, the twins freshly bathed and changed and a sumptuous meal ready for her young husband. It was like something out of Women's Weekly. She had a young husband who was quickly climbing the corporate ladder and even more quickly, leaving his family behind.

Getting ready to go out to another company dinner, Julie was bemoaning the fact that everything felt tight on her. She'd been the same weight and dress size since she was sixteen and had never battled with her weight. The only time she'd been unable to fit into her clothes was...OMG...Good heavens, how could she have missed that? She was absolutely delighted, over the moon, even. Goodness knows how she'd cope, but she would. Maybe it would be a girl this time.

The look on her husband's face when she joyfully told him her suspicions was like a cold hand round her heart.

There must be no more babies, twins were enough. They had to think of the cost of raising another child. No, definitely no more, measures would have to be taken and taken immediately.

How could he even think that she would do what he asked? How could he possibly feel this way? How could she ever have loved this man?

Life was never the same for Julie after that. She was a mere shadow of her former self. She lost interest in everything; the house was never up to Bobby's standards. The twins, although well-fed and clothed, never had that wonderful smell that only babies have. As for her, she was a mess. She gained two stones in weight, spent most of her time in her dressing gown and hated her husband with a passion she didn't know had existed within her. Julie would never forgive him.

There was no chance of them ever having another child. Oh, they kept up a front for the children's sake but had slept in separate rooms since the night she had returned from the clinic. As time went by they co-existed in the same house, but had virtually no communication other than subjects concerning the twins. Bobby had no sympathy for her and found it quite ridiculous that she was still harping on about something that had occurred five years previously, something that had been a mere blip on his career path.

She knew he couldn't bear to look at her. Not that she cared. Where was the smart, well turned-out young mum? She was certainly no credit to him now, and he had reached a peak in his career where a wife or partner was a necessary appendage.

She refused to accompany him to any social events. Not that he would have considered taking such an unkempt, overweight boring companion, who seemed not to bother that he had other company. On the few times he did communicate with her, she was left in no doubt how he felt So it had come as no surprise when he announced he was leaving her.

She was angry, so very angry, angrier than she'd probably ever been. The pompous fool thought he was being so generous, so magnanimous in his offer to provide for her and the boys. Fuck! They were his kids and as for providing for her? Damn right he would, considering the life he had taken from her. But the real nub of her anger was that he had had the gall to tell her he wanted a divorce, a divorce in order to bring up his new family. Yes, he could afford another child now. Well, she'd see about that!

Hell hath no fury like a woman scorned and Julie was that woman. She hired the best lawyer she could and got immense satisfaction in taking Bobby for every penny he had and even some he didn't. But the look of distaste in both his and the floosie's eyes cut her to the quick.

"Gee, she's a horror," whispered the fancy piece.

"What did you ever see in her?"

A horror am I? She vowed no-one would ever look at her like that again. She would have the make-over of all make-overs. Let's face it, she could well afford it. But first she had to try to shift the extra weight.

Kylie

If God wanted us to go on diets, he would have given us willpower.

This had to be her lucky day, a number 44 was waiting for her at the bus stop. There was rather a large queue but she was sure she would get on. It couldn't be the same bus, could it? Elbowing her way to the front she hopped back on amidst roars from the furious onlookers. Oops, she had done it again, bloody stupid place to leave a casualty. Sitting down on the same seat she'd vacated twenty minutes ago, she couldn't believe it, there on the seat was the missing Mars bar. It was serendipity. She was meant to have this last one.

The very last one she promised herself. She would be so good for the next twelve weeks; no Mars bars, no Snickers, no chocolate of any kind. A simple diet of lettuce leaves and a stick of celery, no problem. And she would start first thing tomorrow. Spooky or what? Lying beside the missing sweet was a postcard advertising Fat Fighters. There was a class on Wednesday at 6pm, just five minutes from work. She'd go. Whether it was fate, karma or whatever, she'd go and surprise everyone at how slim she would soon be.

The bus was moving, should she get off at the

chippie or go straight home? She might as well stop at the chippie. There would probably be nothing left at home and after all, it would be her last proper meal for weeks so she had better make the most of it. She would be so good from tomorrow onwards.

Smiling to herself she thought, it's not been such a bad day after all and I'll make it up with everyone tomorrow. Yes, I'll make it up with them all and would even go in half an hour early to get back in Bill's good books. He wasn't really that bad and maybe she had been pushing it a bit. Yes, definitely she'd go in early. Maybe she should take some cakes in, not that she'd eat any, no. She was going to be so good, she had to think 'dress'. But she'd definitely take cakes in to smooth over the cracks with her colleagues. It would look even better if she was being deprived of a luscious cream cake; she'd look really sincere, which of course she was.

Kylie arrived home after her trip to the chip shop and put her tea time treat of cod and chips into the oven to keep warm while she changed and showered. She had, of course, eaten the other portion on the way home. Well, she was late getting home and had almost missed her lunch, then there was the entire trauma on the journey home and it was going to be her last treat. Yes, she was going to be so good from now on.

Selena

I wish I was as thin as I was when I thought I was fat!

Looking round the brightly lit room, she thought, Oh man, this was definitely out of her comfort zone. All those women, and each one bigger than the next. Thank goodness the meeting was on the ground floor, she chuckled.

She'd never been to a club like this before, it just wasn't her thing. But this had to be done, it was imperative, she couldn't fail, she was desperate.

Oh, she knew she wasn't good with diets and she comforted herself that Winston liked a bit of meat on her bones. Most Jamaican men did and she certainly had plenty of meat on her bones. Selena was a big woman, a big woman with a big heart but no willpower.

Every morning in life she promised herself that today was the day. Today she'd start her diet. But a spoonful of bran and half a slice of dry toast just wasn't that appealing. So inevitably, by lunch time the diet was usually over. On a few occasions she made it through the day to dinner. She would be so happy that she'd celebrate by cooking a huge feast of fried chicken (one million calories) or ackies and dumplings (a mere half a million calories) 'cos it just proved she could do it.

But this time it was different. That's why she was

here. This was a one-off and she couldn't let Winston down. He had worked and worked to save the money for this programme, knowing how important it was for her and willpower or no, she wanted a child with all her heart. So somehow she had to find the strength to overcome her weaknesses. She had ninety days to achieve her goal. Only ninety days.

Tearing open the letter she handed it to Winston. "You read it. If it's bad news..."

Taking the paper from his wife, Winston quickly scanned the contents. He shouted with delight "It's not. We're in. We're in!"

Grabbing the letter she roared with laughter and danced around the kitchen, waving it above her head. She laughed and laughed till the tears ran down her cheeks. At long last the chance they had been waiting for was just within their grasp.

"What does it say?" Winston said trying to retrieve it from Selena. "C'mon, what does it say?"

"It says we are about to have a baby, that's what it says. We are going to have a baby and soon," sang his wife. "We're going to have a baby."

"Thank you, God. Thank you. Honestly, I was sure it would be a no. Everything seemed to be against us. Age, weight, lifestyle. I honestly thought it would be a no," Winston marvelled. "I still can't quite believe it."

"Believe it, man. It says it here in black and white. It says Mr and Mrs Winston Buckingham are hereby accepted on an IVF programme. See for yourself," Selena handed the letter back to him.

"I know it's a bit premature to be celebrating, but I say we get the family round, open a bottle of rum and have a party before we get down to the serious business of making a baby." And party they did!

The following day when the euphoria had died down a little, Selena reread the letter and the booklet which came with it. There were loads of do's and dont's, but the one which worried her most was the section about weight. It said categorically in the booklet that the weight limit to start the programme was at least 45lbs lighter than she had been for years. This was bad! How she was going to manage that, she didn't know. But please God, help me make it happen.

Maybe it was fate or karma, but as she turned a page of the magazine on the table in front of her, there was an advert for a new slimming club – FAT FIGHTERS 4 YOU and there was a class starting in two hours, a mere five minute walk from her office.

"Thank you, God."

JULIE

I'm not fat – just easy to see!

Julie wasn't sure about the new class, FAT FIGHTERS 4 YOU. The diet regime had certainly been a huge disappointment. It wasn't new, it was just Fighting Fat rehashed, and she already knew the Bible inside out. In fact, she was sure she had a copy somewhere in the house. Well, she might give it a bash and see how things worked out for the first week, but honestly, she didn't hold out much hope.

Julie felt she needed to be challenged, to be motivated, and in a class that big it was difficult. And if it was difficult for her, who knew all the ropes, how hard would it be for Cheryl, Selena and the other girl (was it Kylie?) to succeed?

What a shame she thought, the three new members really did have an uphill battle and Julie was sure that none of them had actually understood the logistics of the diet and were more than likely to get it wrong and fail. Unless of course they had some help. But in a class this size they had no chance.

Should she lend a hand? Why not? Who better than her? She had more dieting experience than most of the class put together, maybe not successful experience, but why split hairs?

She'd take the newbies under her wing. Yep, that's

precisely what she'd do. They would be Slim Buddies and she would be their mentor. She would motivate them; she would keep them on the dieting straight and narrow. She would guide them to a slimmer world. Julie had a mission.

She was absolutely whacked from work today. It had taken almost two hours longer than usual to get round her collections, and the staff in the post room were not at all happy with her. Was it her fault that so many of the girls wanted to know how she'd got on at the new club? A few of them seemed quite interested in joining, depending on how she and the three amigos got on. Oh yes, she'd told everyone in the building about her Slimming Buddies. Depending on how well her protégés did, it looked like she'd recruited a few more Slim Buddies... She wasn't sure if the three would be annoyed that she had disclosed confidential information to the entire office building; weight and vital statistics.

Knowing Julie's propensity for exaggeration, most of them just wanted to see for themselves. It would be a laugh. Imagine that huge female in IT being that big! God, how did anyone get so enormous? Surely it was against the law?

Julie was regarded as the slimming guru in the office, but unfortunately, only by herself. According to her there was nothing she didn't know about losing weight, or so she thought. Yes, she was the go-to person if someone wanted to lose weight for a party, a holiday or a date. She had the remedy. She knew how to lose twenty pounds in a weekend and how to fit into a party dress in seven days. The trouble was, as far as losing weight herself went, she had the theory down pat but the practicalities left much to be desired.

She had for some time harboured a secret desire to be a class consultant. She knew she could inspire great losses and her goal was to one day have a class of her own. She could see herself standing on the podium in her dark blue suit with all the little gold bars on the lapel. She wasn't quite sure what they represented, but she'd have loads of them. Yes, she would have the best class in the country. There would be a waiting list to become a member. People would actually put on weight so that they could join. No doubt about it, Julie would be the most inspirational mentor ever. She couldn't be anything else, she'd seen them all, the best and the worst.

There was only one thing that stood between her and her goal, and that was Julie. She had to attain her target weight and although it wasn't for the want of trying, she was still a long way off.

So perhaps she exaggerated a little, it was simply encouragement. Okay, so she had a bit more than a lettuce for lunch and she hadn't run 5K. The reality was she'd walked quickly in the rain to pick up a happy meal. She really was going to start practising what she preached tomorrow. Tonight it would be a nice glass of Lambrini, and on hearing the doorbell, she knew dinner had arrived.

"Pizza delivery."

She would start in earnest tomorrow.

SELENA

From: julie.simpson@unicorp.com
To: selena.buckingham@unicorp.com
cc: cheryl.mason@unicorp.com
Subject: START AS YOU MEAN TO GO ON
Morning girlies just finished breakfast – 2 vitamin pills and a cup of black tea.

Burn that lot off running into work.

See ya

Julie

-o0o-

From: selena.buckingham@unicorp.com
To: julie.simpson@unicorp.com
Subject: START AS YOU MEAN TO GO ON
Just did!!! Run to work!! You're having a laugh I just saw your car pass the end of my street.

2 vitamin pills? Give it a rest.

-o0o-

Breakfast was the most important meal of the day, or so the Bible says.

One banana spread on one slice of toast (no butter) and a cup of black tea. Oh, my Lord, she couldn't wait for lunch. This wasn't breakfast, this was what Selena would snack on while making breakfast, and as far as she was concerned every meal was important.

How was she going to cope? She'd faint, she'd pass out, and she couldn't survive on this minuscule intake of food, especially whilst frying crispy maple bacon, tomatoes and a couple of eggs sunny side up for Winston. God, she was actually drooling and sneakily dipping a tiny bit of crust into the hot sizzling frying pan. She burned her finger.

"Ouch," she yelped.

"You okay?"

"Yes fine, just a splash of hot fat."

"Hope you're not sneaking a bit," Winston joked.

God, was he psychic?

"Don't be so nasty, of course I'm not sneaking anything, I'M ON A DIET," she roared as she flipped one of the eggs absent-mindedly.

Damn, he hated them flipped. Too bad, he shouldn't have been so mean. Gazing lovingly at the egg, she was tempted, sorely tempted – she could always do him another. Who would know? She loved fried eggs; she loved fried eggs and tomatoes even more and there was plenty. No, if she couldn't get past breakfast she had no chance. Slapping the meal on the table she called to Winston to hurry before the food got cold. What she really meant was, hurry before I scoff the lot.

Surprisingly she'd enjoyed the Slimming Club last night. It wasn't at all like she had expected. Everyone was very friendly and encouraging and her big dread that someone would shout out her weight for all to hear didn't happen, of course. She didn't even mind the two from the office turning up. Julie was obviously a veteran, a season ticket holder of the Slimming Club world. She appeared to know everyone including the counsellor and she knew the 'Bible' inside out. For someone so dedicated, Julie wasn't exactly sylph-like, for all her expertise.

The Fat Fighters diet wasn't as Julie had been led to believe. She'd been under the impression that this was the latest diet to do the circuit, as it seemed did many of the attendees. Not merely an old diet rehashed. How many new diets could there be? pondered Selena but it was new to her, and to the girl from the IT department, Chloe, or Claire, she couldn't for the life of her remember the girl's name.

She knew her by sight because they both worked for the same company. But Cheryl (that was her name) didn't fraternise with any of her colleagues. She didn't hang out with any of the younger ones which was a shame – there were always nights out clubbing or barbeques. In fact, social life within the firm seemed to take preference over work for some of them.

This kid seemed a real loner. Strange, for all she was a big girl, she was certainly not visible at work. Selena wouldn't have been surprised if few of their workmates actually recognised her. She got behind her screen in the morning and hardly moved until the end of the day. Had it not been for the debris - the

46

litter of food and drinks - it would have looked like no-one worked there. Well, she hoped for her sake that the slimming club worked; Cheryl could be quite pretty if she tried.

Although Selena had enjoyed the camaraderie of the club, unfortunately the maths didn't work. She had to lose a huge amount of weight before the programme started and according to the counsellor, members, if they really worked hard, could lose on average 2lb a week which would take her 175 days, way over her time limit, she had under 100 days to reach her target weight. Selena was going to have to find another way.

Four newbies had enrolled the previous night, three of them from the same firm and a young dour lass who seemed totally uninterested in what was going on. In fact Selena wondered why on earth she was there, but it takes all types, she laughed to herself.

Cheryl

I only eat in three places: here. there. and everywhere.

Lunchtime. God she was starving, but where was her lunch, what had she done with it? Where had it gone? She had got up half an hour earlier this morning to make her sandwiches, exactly as illustrated in the book, (or the bible as the slimmers called it), together with a bag of low fat crisps, a fat-free yoghurt and a chocolate bar at 99 calories for tea break. It was all in the preparation.

What was the old saying: "Fail to Prepare and Prepare to Fail."

She had prepared, she had been meticulous, but the Tupperware box was empty. Okay, she'd had the chocolate bar with her coffee at half ten and, feeling a bit peckish, half the sandwich with a few crisps at eleven, but where were the rest of her goodies? Somebody had nicked them.

This had happened loads of times, Cheryl would buy a couple of sandwiches or a cake for her break and when she went to get them they were gone. She was convinced it was that miserable, skinny cow Sandy – stick of celery Sandy who never brought anything in for lunch and seldom left her desk. She had to be pinching other people's lunch, it stood to reason.

It hadn't bothered Cheryl that much before. Oh, she'd get a bit mad if her strawberry tart disappeared, but she would simply go and buy another. In fact, she'd got into the habit of buying two of everything in case one did get pinched, and it was such a bonus if the thief was having a day off.

But today was different. She was on a diet and she had to carefully weigh everything and count the calories she was allowed to consume in a day. Here she was on day one and some rotten devil had scuppered her schedule. What was she going to do for lunch? Nothing else for it, she'd have to nip out for something, no way could she last till tea time.

The queue was miles long and by the time it was Cheryl's turn, the shop had sold out of all the diet stuff. It had! Mmm, a BLT, now that was slimming. It was salad and grilled bacon: that wasn't too fattening. She'd also have extra coleslaw on the side, which was only cabbage and stuff. Mayonnaise wasn't that bad, and a Granola bar (they were made with nuts and stuff, healthy eating) and a diet coke.

Back at her desk with her second lunch of the day and feeling a bit guilty, she checked the calorie value of her purchases. She opened the Bible. OMG! The sandwich was 500 calories. The Granola Bar was 235 and the coleslaw – Luxury American Deli – was 200 calories per 100 grams. That was about another 300, a total of 1035 calories. She was only allowed 1000 a day and she had gone over that with this lot alone. She'd had 250 at breakfast (450) and that was without dinner or supper.

Well, she was starving and she had paid for this lot, so no way was it going to waste. Nothing else for it, she'd start again tomorrow.

From: julie.simpson@unicorp.com
To: selena.buckingham@unicorp.com
cc: cheryl.mason@unicorp.com
Just had a whole lettuce for lunch – 10 calories and a bottle of water – 0 calories. 5k run – feel fantastic.

KYLIE

From: julie.simpson@unicorp.com
To: kylie.harper@hofmail.com
Subject: JUST BELIEVE!!
Just do what it says in the bible and you'll get your rewards.
Running into work – join me?

-o0o-

From: kylie.harper@hofmail.com
To: julie.simpson@unicorp.com
Subject: JUST BELIEVE!!
Who the fuck are you?

-o0o-

From: julie.simpson@unicorp.com
To: kylie.harper@hofmail.com
Subject: JUST BELIEVE!!
Julie from the slimming club.

-o0o-

From: kylie.harper@hofmail.com
To: julie.simpson@unicorp.com
Subject: JUST BELIEVE!!
How did you get my email address and no, I don't want to run into work! I've been at work for ages.

-o0o-

What a disappointment the slimming club had turned out to be: two pounds a week. Bloody hell, it would take her about a year and a half to get anywhere near fitting into 'The Dress'. No, that was no good, absolutely useless. She hadn't for a moment realised there would be dozens and dozens of fat people all crammed into this teensy little hall. She kind of thought she would have her own slimming consultant who would somehow be at her beck and call. Not standing in a queue a mile long to be weighed and lied to. Yes, the woman had had the audacity to lie straight to her face. The scales were wrong, never in her life had she been that weight and she damned well wasn't now. Come on, if you couldn't trust the scales what was the point of being there?

Then there was the nutty woman who'd sat down beside her with her two friends. Who the devil was she? Making her fill in a form and assuring her she could easily lose up to a stone this first week; something about watermelon retention and ketones. And if she stuck to what it said in the bible, she would be fine and lose loads.

The bible? She wasn't sure if there was still one in the house. She used to go to Sunday school, but that was years ago and even if she could find one, what part were you supposed to read? Just start at the beginning? If she remembered rightly it had millions of pages. Or was it a choice of the Old or the New Testament? There was a bit where an old guy built a boat and took loads and loads of animals to make sure he could feed his family.

Or was it where Jesus did magic when he turned water into wine? That would be great at parties. Or feeding loads of folk on bread and fish? No way was she going near fish, not with her job. And the bread, wasn't that full of carbs? Maybe that's where the praying came in, you prayed that there was nothing fattening, no calories in your food. But surely that was a bit random? What if God was busy and wasn't listening? You could end up fatter than when you started. No, she didn't think this club was for her. A fiver a week to become a Christian? Alright, maybe you'd be a thin Christian, but it wasn't for her.

She still hadn't broken the news to Mum and the boys that they had to stump up nine hundred quid for the dress. She wasn't quite as confident in the cold light of day that they would hand over the lolly without a fight, but she had ways of making them pay. It might take a little persuasion, but she'd have her own way in the end, she always did.

Jason and Mandy hadn't been around; something about a school reunion. Strange that, they had attended different schools, in fact, they were brought up in different parts of the country. Hmmm, something smelled fishy. Oh, it was probably her.

Let's see if this bible thingy worked. She would just open it up at any page and see what it said.

After fasting forty days and forty nights, he was hungry.

SPOOKY!   And she was complaining about missing her lunch. Wow. Well, she'd give this a try.

Stopping off at McDonald's she ordered a chocolate milkshake and a double quarter pounder with fries and a McFlurry. Hey, if this worked she would be one happy girl.

So, out in the car park, away from prying eyes, she was all set to do the next bit, the magic part.

Closing her eyes and sort of kneeling down by the picnic tables, she started her prayers.

"Hello God, it's Kylie here." When she heard the voice she almost passed out.

"Kylie?" My God, that was quick...someone was calling to her, was she the chosen one?

She'd always known she was different, was special, and now she had the proof. Here was God himself talking to her.

"OMG, it's her, look! There, kneeling down at the picnic tables. She must have lost a chip. Quick, disappear. Don't let her see you," whispered the voice of her best friend.

It wasn't God, it was Mandy, but what was she doing here and who was she with? mused Kylie.

She hoped the spell had worked and the food would not have any calorific value, but she doubted it.

"How could you know where I'd be?" Kylie puzzled. "I just made up my mind a few minutes ago."

"Kylie, where else would you be at feeding time? Of course you'd be here."

"Don't say a word to anybody, especially Jason. Where is he, by the way?"

"No idea," replied Mandy, but she was ever so shifty.

"Anyway, I'm on this diet. You can eat whatever you like, but you have to do what's in the Bible."

"EH?" said Mandy. "Rubbish! You're telling me you can eat all that lot and still lose weight?"

"Yep, I go to this club and they're all on it. Honest, all they talk about is the Bible this and the Bible that and I'm telling you it works."

"So how much have you lost then?" quizzed her best friend.

"Nothing yet, I've just started it. Look, look who's coming. Jason. Hey! Jason, I'm here, over here with Mandy. What are you doing here?"

"I came to find you."

"But how did you know where to look?"

"It's feeding time, where else would you be?" Jason replied.

Kylie

From: julie.simpson@unicorp.com
To: kylie.harper@hofmail.com
Subject: HAPPY BIRTHDAY
Remember be a winner not a sinner
Enjoy your day
Luv Julie

-o0o-

From: kylie.harper@hofmail.com
To: julie.simpson@unicorp.com
Subject: HAPPY BIRTHDAY
Piss off

-o0o-

Snuggling back under the covers, Kylie was more than reluctant to get up. She could surely have another half hour and still catch the bus? Oh, just another fifteen minutes, she'd catch the next one and still be able to clock in on time. Damn, she would never catch the 7.40 and you could never rely on getting on the next one. Maybe Ma would drive her in? After all it was her birthday. She dashed about her room while gazing at 'The Dress'. She'd collected it on Saturday and hadn't been able to take her eyes off it since. Late or not, she still had time to daydream as she pictured herself dancing with Jason at the ball, looking fantastic. Jason was just about to go down on one knee when her mother bellowed at her to get a move on as she was going to be late again.

She quickly jumped on the scales to check how well she was doing, just a quick peek. WHAT!!!! No, that couldn't possibly be right. 2lbs on!! No! No chance, she'd been ultra-good yesterday, they had to be wrong. Definitely they were wrong, she thought as she moved them round the bathroom.

She just couldn't find 'THAT' place, the place where you always weighed lighter. Nope, they still read 2lbs on. She needed to buy a new set; these old ones were obviously buggered. She gave them a mighty kick, sending them clear across the bathroom floor. She'd have to buy new ones now. No time to brood, it was her birthday and she didn't care what the stupid scales said, Kylie was going to have a day off from dieting. Pity she couldn't have a proper day off, everyone had a day off on their birthday.

Grabbing a slice of toast and tearing open the paper on her presents, she pleaded with her mother to give her a run into work. God, if she was late again this week she really would be for the high jump.

Reluctantly her mum agreed and she arrived bang on time. But guess who was standing waiting? Yes, Bill. And he looked quite miffed; if she didn't know better she'd think he was annoyed she had been on time. Why? Why on earth would he want her to be late? Hey ho, whatever his evil master plan, she'd thwarted him. C'mon it was her birthday, and nothing could go wrong on this special day.

Cheryl

From: julie.simpson@unicorp.com
To: selena.buckingham@unicorp.com
cc: cheryl.mason@unicorp.com
cc: kylie.harper@hofmail.com
Subject: LADIES WHO LUNCH
How about a few laps round the park? Sugar-free gum and waterproofs.

-o0o-

Reply from: kylie.harper@hofmail.com
Subject: LADIES WHO LUNCH
Been out – done three circuits – off to church for communion – no calories left (bread & wine)

-o0o-

Reply from: cheryl.mason@unicorp.com
Subject: LADIES WHO LUNCH
Sorry already signed up for Boot Camp – lose 5lb a day and before you ask, the class is full.

-o0o-

Reply from: selena.buckingham@unicorp.com
Subject: LADIES WHO LUNCH
Sugar free gum?
Laps round park?
Going to church?
Gimme a break!!!!

-o0o-

Cheryl hated lying, but no way was she going to let on she hadn't actually started yet. She was only a bit behind and she'd soon catch up. Today was the day, she had everything under control. Lunch sorted; snacks sorted; dinner was in the slow cooker, ready for when she got home. Yes, she had everything in order and no way was anyone going to help themselves to her lunch today, she'd make sure of that. Cheryl was really excited and upbeat, and so determined to succeed this time. She could see herself in a fabulous white gown just like Kim Kardashian.

Because she'd screwed up her eating yesterday she had seen no reason to deprive herself of dinner; may as well get hung for a sheep as a lamb. So her very last meal had been her absolute favourite. An Indian banquet for two. Usually she'd leave some for the following night, but it seemed such a shame to waste all that delicious food. After all, she couldn't finish it off tomorrow, she'd be on her diet.

By the time Doug had signed on, Cheryl had finished the banquet for two, the remainder of a tin of Roses, demolished a couple of bags of crisps (family size) and topped that lot off with a carton of Ben & Jerry's, the cookie dough was to die for. My God, she was fit to burst.

Oh, she felt sick, really sick and Doug was being so sympathetic. Maybe it was something she'd eaten, he suggested. Damned tootin' it was. She'd scoffed the equivalent of a day's food for six people; of course she felt sick. She couldn't possibly confess. The reason was that he saw Cheryl, his beloved bride-to-be, as a well-stacked femme fatale, not a fatal femme or heart attack waiting to happen.

Well, that had been yesterday and today was a new day and a new start. Breakfast was a couple of laxatives, a lightly boiled egg and a cup of green tea. Green tea? Yuck! She hated all that muck. Tea should be black, no other colour and if it was, it wasn't tea. An egg, just one teeny wee egg. Once she'd mashed it up in a cup with a smidgeon of butter (there was no way that could do any harm), the egg was gone and that was breakfast. Wandering around the kitchen looking for food that had no calories proved futile. Good Lord above, the laxative was beginning to work. Her internal plumbing was making the most peculiar gurgling noises. Taking laxatives after a vindaloo was probably not the most sensible thing to do. OMG.

Goodness, she might not have stuck to the diet, but she sure as hell had just lost weight, and she didn't think she was going to make it to work. She couldn't move more than ten yards from the loo and it felt like this was going to be a very unpleasant morning. Oh, God, here we go again. She dashed through the house.

A phone call to work and she was free for the remainder of the day. But something was needed to stop this awful predicament. When she was little and had had any kind of tummy upset, her mother would feed her and her brother boiled eggs, or copious amounts of steamed rice. "To bind you," Mum had said. Well, she'd had one egg for breakfast so another few should do the trick, and it wouldn't really be mucking up the diet. Certainly not the way her digestive system was working.

So, four boiled eggs and six slices of bread and butter later the problem had alleviated somewhat. But she was still a little fragile. The other cure for her problem was rice, steamed rice. On opening her store cupboard she discovered that she had no rice, but wow, she did have a family-size tin of creamed rice. Her favourite, just warmed up with a teaspoon of jam. One family-size tin and half a jar of strawberry jam later, she was feeling much better. Shame about the diet, but it couldn't be helped and she definitely couldn't have worked in that condition. Talking about the diet, she might as well have her packed lunch, no use in wasting it. So, by ten am she'd had five boiled eggs, half a loaf of bread with butter, a huge tin of rice and loads of jam, a couple of sandwiches, a packet of low fat crisps, an apple and a banana. Thank God she wasn't feeling too good, if that's what she ate when she felt poorly...

Cheryl ate and slept for most of the day, a sandwich here and a little cake there, just to keep her strength up. So by the time it came for her to hook up with Doug she wasn't feeling too clever, for the second night running. He was the kindest and most considerate man in the universe. Nothing was too much trouble;

she should go and make some ginger tea, that would help her. Why not drink some cola? His mom swore by it. Just stir in some sugar and drink it flat, works every time. She was too dim to realise he wasn't actually doing anything, just issuing orders, and if he only knew that the last thing she needed was more of anything. What she needed was to give her body a complete rest from food and drink. She needed to detox and God above, if the pong in the loo was anything to go by, well enough said.

Tomorrow would be different; she'd start properly tomorrow.

Julie

What do you call people who watch other people diet?
Weight watchers.

Julie loved her job, she knew it didn't take Einstein to push a post cart from office to office, but she loved it and it made her feel important. Everyone knew Julie and even if most of them thought she was a bit dim, or daft as a brush, it was her they went to if they needed information, or help, and it was usually she who came up trumps. However, if you wanted to keep something under wraps, or confidential, she was not your girl.

Everything about everybody eventually came through the post room, ergo through Julie. So, long before a person knew they were being promoted, or in some cases, demoted, Julie knew well in advance. She was also privy, from time to time, to information that was not for general consumption. She knew what was simply water-cooler stuff and that was okay. But sometimes she got to know something that she wished she didn't, and this was one of them.

The company, it appeared, was the subject of a hostile takeover bid and it looked like they were all possibly going to be out of a job if it succeeded. Wow, this was not good, but she knew she couldn't just go blabbing to all and sundry. But this was big news and concerned them all, what was she going to do?

First of all she needed to find out a bit more about who was staging the takeover. The company in the frame was an asset-stripping outfit based in Philadelphia. The CEO was some mysterious figure named Douglas Winthrop III. There was very little known about him, a recluse who had built up a massive fortune by buying and stripping companies globally. No information on his private life either, he certainly was no play boy, according to the information she'd gathered. He might well be some nerd sitting in his bedroom at night, online to other like-minded nerds. The only difference being, he had three or four billion dollars to his name.

SELENA

You're either too fat or too thin. You just can't win.

Selena and Winston were an extremely sociable couple who entertained family and friends regularly. Any excuse for a get-together and it was open house. For them life was all about lots of fun and good company and of course, good food. Selena was renowned for her mountains of wonderful, delicious food and last night had been no exception. Except, she had been miserable. She had been restricted to a couple of rice cakes. Rice cakes that looked like inedible table mats smeared with a low calorie, tasteless spread. They not only looked like table mats, although never having had the pleasure, they were what she imagined table mats would taste like. It was really hard to play the perfect hostess, having a whale of a time dishing out her mouth-watering goodies for seconds and even thirds.

She had encouraged her guests to have a tiny bit more. "Oh, go on" she'd said, "enjoy yourself, just have a little taste. I'm sure you'll like it." All the while abstaining herself, resisting temptation and starving. Of course she had been well aware that she wasn't starving; she was hungry, yes, but starving, no.

Standing in the kitchen with an almost empty platter Selena had toyed with the last piece of chicken. Surely one piece of chicken wouldn't do any harm?

Just one succulent piece, she had been so good and so strict over the past few days. Counting the calories in every morsel she consumed; being sorely tempted but not succumbing, she had been so proud of herself.

But this, this was too much. It couldn't do that much harm and she'd promised herself she'd work it off tomorrow. She'd go with those other nut jobs to the gym (not that she believed for one minute that they actually did go), but she would go and subject herself to all kinds of torture if she could just have this last piece.

Just as she was about to succumb, about to give in to temptation, Winston had walked in and grabbed, yes, grabbed, the chicken in question. Selena had almost burst out crying. She was furious, foot-stampingly furious. How dare he? HOW BLOODY DARE HE? He'd snatched her chicken; he had actually taken the food from her mouth.

"What's up babe?" he had asked, smacking her derrière.

"WHATS UP?" She had bellowed. "What's up? You inconsiderate moron! You come in here stealing food and ask me what's up?"

"Eh?" was all he could muster, looking at her as though she'd grown horns?

"Eh? Stealing food? A moron? Ah ha, you were going to eat that last bit," he chuckled.

"No, I was not," she replied. You know I'm on a diet."

"You were going to eat it. You were, and I saved you. PRAISE THE LORD, I SAVED YOU," he had sung and pranced round the kitchen.

"Don't be such an idiot, that piece of chicken you saved me from was going straight in the bin; the dog had just sicked it up, smartarse."

"We don't have a dog," he roared with laughter. "You were going to sneak it for yourself." Backing out of the kitchen he had called above the general racket, "Hey, everybody, watch out for the dog, he's stealing food."

"Dog? I didn't know they had a dog."

"When did you get a dog Winston?"

"Does it bite?" Another queried.

"Only chickens," said Winston.

Selena was mortified but she knew she'd been well and truly caught out and had the good grace to take it on the chin. Hey, and maybe it was fate or karma that had sent Winston into the kitchen. But all that, for one small piece of chicken?

From: julie.simpson@unicorp.com
To: selena.buckingham@unicorp.com
cc: cheryl.mason@unicorp.com
cc: kylie.harper@hofmail.com
Subject: I'M FREE
Morning girlies – anyone for gym session – free admission today only.

Lunch – two pickled onions and seaweed infusion.

-o0o-

Reply from; cheryl.mason@unicorp.com
Subject: I'M FREE
Get a life!

-o0o-

Reply from: selena.buckingham@unicorp.com
Not a chance.

-o0o-

Reply from: kylie.harper@hofmail.com
Piss off

-o0o-

What was today's 'message of hope,' as she had christened Julie's 'words of encouragement'? What rubbish was she spouting this morning?

Selena almost fell off the bed laughing, the woman was mad. She was probably tucking into a full fat latte and a bacon and egg sandwich. As for the gym, the only machine she was familiar with in the gym was the vending machine.

Selena was back on form, the chicken forgotten. It was going to be a good day. It didn't matter how crap the table mats tasted, she would stick with them. She just had to remember what she had to gain.

CHERYL

Every girl's dream is to find the perfect guy... pshhh,
every girl's dream is to eat without getting fat!

Cheryl was mesmerized by her ring, it was simply the most beautiful ring she had ever seen. It had three large stones surrounded by heaven knows how many baguettes, set in silver, not that she had any knowledge of jewellery. She thought it was probably zirconium from the sheer size and number of stones, but she didn't care. It was beautiful and it was hers.

Doug had planned the whole proposal with great precision. The parcel had arrived the day before and he had given her strict instructions not to open it until he said. The package was to be unwrapped when he came online and he would talk her through his surprise. Getting down on one knee, he told her to open the box. There it was, her absolutely fabulous ring.

Unfortunately, it was more than a bit tight and she had had a devil of a job to get it off later that night. She had been frightened at one stage that it would have to be cut off, but she had finally managed it.

There was nothing for it, she'd have to get it resized and quickly. Doug was bound to notice she wasn't wearing it.

Entering the jeweller's shop, she was surprised at the enthusiastic welcome she received from the little man, Mr Cohen, as he introduced himself. She had dealt with him a few times over the past couple of months when Doug had sent her other gifts. She had to admit her fiancé had the most exquisite taste. After a few pleasantries Cheryl took the box from her bag and handed it to Mr Cohen.

The jeweller's eyes lit up, the name on the box was obviously known to him.

"Van Cleef & Arpels. Hmmm, this should be something," he murmured to himself. He actually let out a gasp when he saw what the box contained.

"Beautiful, isn't it?" Cheryl asked him. "I've never seen anything like it."

"Nor I," he answered.

"I'm hoping you can make it bigger. I know you don't usually do costume jewellery, but this ring is very special."

"Yes you're right there, but what do you mean about costume jewellery?"

"This. My engagement ring. I think its zirconium and silver, but it's just too tight. It makes my finger swell."

"Zirconium and silver? Why would you think it was zirconium and silver? Am I missing something? It's not stolen, is it?"

"No it is not!" she retorted. "Heavens, if these were real diamonds it would be worth a king's ransom. Of course it's zirconium, but I love it just the same."

"My dear girl you've brought some fabulous pieces

in before – the Cartier bracelet and the Patek Phillipe watch were something, but this? This is beyond fabulous. The cut and clarity of the stones is exquisite, not to mention the size and the fact it is set in platinum and made by one of the most famous jewellers in the world. You are one lucky girl."

"I am, I know, but can you fix it?" Cheryl asked.

"This ring would have to go back to Van Cleef & Arpel, we couldn't undertake such a commission. I don't think any jeweller would. Have you any idea what this ring is worth?"

"No, I just loved it and as I said, it couldn't be worth any more to me if it was twenty five carats of diamonds and set in platinum. The value doesn't really matter."

"I think you are in for a bit of a shock."

"I'm not, honestly it doesn't matter if it's only worth a tenner, it means everything to me."

"You weren't listening earlier were you? This ring is fabulous."

Cheryl was beginning to get a bit agitated, she had to get back to work soon. She was on her lunch break and her tummy was growling in protest; she was finding it hard to concentrate.

"At a rough estimate, I would say two fifty. Maybe a little more, but two fifty wouldn't be far off the mark."

"As much as that? That's okay, but why can't you fix it for me? I need it done, like now."

"No way!" exclaimed Mr Cohen. "As I said, this

ring would have to go back to the original designer. I wouldn't even attempt to make adjustments."

"But you've got rings in your case for £500 up to £1000 so why would this be so out of the question?"

"You're right, but do you see any priced at quarter of a million?"

"Eh! No!"

"My point exactly."

"What has that got to do with my ring?"

"Your ring is worth at least a quarter of a million pounds."

She was a big girl to pick up off the floor.

Selena

From: julie.simpson@unicorp.com
To: selena.buckingham@unicorp.com
cc: cheryl.mason@unicorp.com
cc: kylie.harper@hofmail.com
Subject: POWER OF POSITIVE THINKING
Morning girlies
New miracle diet – lose 5lbs a day – I'm positive it works.

-o0o-

Reply from: selena.buckingham@unicorp.com
Subject: POWER OF POSITIVE THINKING
I'm positive that's the one Janice from accounts has been on – lost positively loads of weight.

-o0o-

Reply from: kylie.harper@hofmail.com
Subject: POWER OF POSITIVE THINKING
Are you positive it was as much as 5lbs a day?

-o0o-

Reply from: selena.buckingham@unicorp.com
Subject: POWER OF POSITIVE THINKING
Not absolutely positive but I'll ask her when she gets out of hospital.

-o0o-

Every month for the past five or six years Selena had gone through the same ritual and always with just a glimmer of hope. As she did every month she would carefully pick her way through the delicate hand-knitted garments she had created over the years. Touching and snuggling them before returning them back to the drawer. Maybe next month.

Selena knew she had to keep positive, she had to be strong and most of all not let either herself or Winston down. He was such a good man. He had worked so hard to save the money for the programme, so it was up to her to get herself fit and lose as much weight as she could. Hey, it was easier said than done.

The past few days she had spent most of her free time on the internet looking for ways to lose weight and my goodness, they ranged from the sublime to the ridiculous. She discounted any that meant swallowing pills or potions. She was afraid that even if they did work some residue could remain in her blood stream and affect her chances of conceiving. No, they had to be natural remedies.

According to Google and Yahoo there were hundreds and hundreds of diets. Ranging from the 'take this Magic Berry and eat what you like forever' to 'Sing yourself thin'. Shame she was tone deaf.

After hours of trawling she was sure she'd struck gold and come up with the solution to her problems. She had stumbled on the latest celebrity fad 'The Oxford Lighter Life' schedule. This revolutionary

'Lose 10lb a week every week for the next three months' diet was just what she was looking for. This fantastic new weight loss control had dozens and dozens of rave reviews from many top celebrities. It must work if they were on it. Mustn't it?

The captions read:

"Lost 40lbs in the first month"
"Can't believe how easy this is"
"I would recommend this to my worst enemy!"
"Wedding dress fitted in just three weeks"
"This was the miracle cure I've had been looking for."

The word miracle was exactly what she wanted. Yes, a miracle would do for her.

Her daily intake for the first month was two cereal bars which tasted like sawdust coated with laxative and a disgusting bowl of porridge, all of which cost an arm and leg for the privilege.

Maybe it was lose £10 a week and not 10lbs? No, that didn't work. It actually cost £60 a week, all payable upfront of course. So here she was, it had just gone 11am on her first day and she had already eaten her two chocolate bars and had nothing left till dinner this evening except water. Who the hell had said it was too easy? No wonder they would recommend it to their worst enemy! She felt squeamish and light-headed. This was absolute torture and only the first day. She had another ninety nine to go. No chance, but she'd spent almost £300 on her month's supply, she had to carry on.

She needed something to take her mind off her plight. Maybe she should go meet up with Julie at the gym? She didn't believe a word the daft devil uttered, but it would be better than staring at everyone eating.

Selena somehow got through the day, but by the time she got home was almost fainting with hunger. She had been so hungry she had eaten the disgusting bowl of slops before she had even taken her coat off, and she was still starving.

Refusing to cook for Winston, she knew this was going to be a long night. Still, it was weigh-in day tomorrow and by heavens, she must have lost a few pounds. She was in bed by 7pm, much to her husband's disgust, but she hoped she could sleep away her hunger pangs. She couldn't. At 2.30am she was in the kitchen with a cheese and pickle sandwich, a glass of milk and two chocolate bars, not the ones covered in laxative.

She'd try again tomorrow.

THE WEIGH-IN

Inside every fat person is a thin person trying to get out.
But they can usually be sedated with a large piece of chocolate cake.

The slimming class was really busy − more and more would-be skinnies had joined this week. Amazing the number of new recruits there were from work, mused Selena. In fact, it was a bit like a works night out.

To save time and get the class under way, Julie had been co-opted to get the newbies enrolled as fast as she could. However, with Julie in charge it took probably twice as long as she welcomed and chatted to each newcomer.

"Gosh, was she cock of the walk?" laughed Selena, nudging Cheryl. "My God, she'll be even more unbearable than usual, and what about those emails she's been sending? She must think we're all mad."

"I just write rubbish back," giggled Cheryl. "Whatever she says, I say I've done better. I'm sure she means well."

"I didn't know who she was," interrupted Kylie. "Getting all those religious messages was spooking me out. Mind you, if they work it'll be the best diet I've ever known."

"Religious messages? What has religion got to

do with anything?" Cheryl and Selena spoke at the same time.

"I didn't get any religious messages from her," said Cheryl.

"Why would you?" Selena queried.

"Here," said Kylie. "Have a butchers," handing over her phone.

Scrolling down through Julie's messages Selena burst out laughing. "I'm not sure who's the daftest," she giggled, handing the phone to Cheryl who also began laughing uproariously.

"What's funny? C'mon tell me what's funny. I did exactly what she told me to do," Kylie wasn't at all pleased. "She told me that as long as I did what it said in the Bible I would be okay."

"The bible, that's the joke. This is the bible." Selena chuckled, holding up the dieting handbook. Everyone calls this the Bible because everything you need to know about the diet is in here."

"So this week has been a total waste of time? Going to communion and praying at the drop of a hat or at the drop of a digestive biscuit and, Good Lord, eating for fun! Just because that crazy mad woman stuck her oar in and misled me," Kylie sulked.

"Oh c'mon now, she didn't do it on purpose, she didn't mean any harm. She thought she was motivating you. Just don't pay any attention to her in future," said Cheryl.

"So you think she's alright do you? You think it's

okay for her to blab to everyone? You don't think it's strange that all these people you both work with have turned up tonight?" posed Kylie.

"Blab? What could she blab about?" retorted Selena.

"And how would you know anyway? Cheryl asked.

"I overheard a couple of them talking in the loo," said Kylie. "They were having a good old laugh."

"They came to see Julie's girls. Yes, Julie's girls. There's Chunky Monkey Cheryl and Nearly Due Selena. I didn't hear what they were calling me, but it sure wouldn't be complimentary," spat out Kylie.

"WHAT?" said Selena through gritted teeth. "That two-faced pain in the arse. I'll give her Nearly Due Selena! How could she be so cruel?" The big woman's eyes filled with tears, but she was damned if she was going to let anyone see how upset she was. Revenge is a dish best supped cold, and she'd get her revenge.

"I DON'T BELIEVE IT!" Cheryl roared. "That's it, this isn't the first time this sort of thing has happened to me. I'm off. I cannot believe that interfering busy body...I could throttle her."

Just at that moment, a couple of the girls from the sales department came sidling across and asked if they could join them, despite there being lots of empty seats elsewhere.

"Sorry girls, these are reserved," answered Kylie. "Unless you need reinforced chairs? Mmm, looking at you, you're probably borderline. Right enough, maybe you shouldn't take a chance. Yes, you sit here beside us but don't move about too much."

They were off like a shot, not wanting to be classed as requiring strengthened seating. No, these two weren't for sitting with the 'Big Girls'.

"That got rid of them," Kylie smirked.

"Listen girls, I've been thinking," said Selena. "Why are we bothering about what a bunch of skinny smart-arses are saying? We are big. We wouldn't be here if we weren't. If you were five stones lighter, Cheryl, they wouldn't dream of calling you names. You're the best-looking person in here, but hey, you need to lose weight. I'm the same. I love my food and it shows, but my husband and I are desperate to start a family and we can't. I can't start the IVF treatment 'til I lose hundreds of pounds. And you, Kylie, you must want to be smaller or you wouldn't be here. So bugger the lot of them, let's stick together and show them."

"What about Julie?" questioned the two younger girls?

"Bugger Julie as well," enthused Selena. "If she wants to spend her time sending us stupid messages, let her carry on. The way to show them all is for us to succeed."

"You're blinking right," said Kylie. "Let's show them," thinking she might as well get a fish supper on the way home. If she'd done well and she thought she might have, then it was a celebration, and if she'd had a rubbish week then commiserations. Yes, fish, chips and mushy peas. She was drooling at the thought.

"I never knew you were desperate to have a family," Cheryl addressed Selena.

"Why would you? It's not something I broadcast, and I certainly don't want all and sundry knowing my business. Remember, if the bosses find out I could be for the high jump".

"They can't do that can they?" posed Cheryl. "Surely they can't get rid of you for being pregnant?"

"Look, girl, they can do what the devil they like. There's no sentiment in business and believe me, there are cutbacks coming, there are all sorts of rumours going around. I'm relying on you to keep schtum."

"Of course, I won't breathe a word, but rumours? What rumours?" Cheryl asked. "I've never heard any rumours."

"That's because you never come out from behind that screen, that's why," laughed Selena. "Nobody knows for real what's happening, but something is going on and you can bet your life our little friend over there knows what. The post room always knows first what's happening."

It was the moment of truth. Selena was pleased as punch with her 6lb weight loss and Cheryl, despite her pig-out, had lost 3lbs. Kylie was going to have to pray a lot harder – she had gained 3lbs, and Julie came bouncing over with the news that she'd stayed the same weight.

Despite Selena's warning and dying to confront

Julie, Cheryl suggested the four of them go for a skinny latte to celebrate, or commiserate, as the case may be. So off they trooped to the nearest coffee shop.

Settled down in the comfy sofas, Julie was all ready to give her little pep talk. But she was cut short by Cheryl who seemed not too pleased; in fact she looked like she was going to throttle someone. It couldn't be her, she hadn't done anything. Well, not that they knew of.

"What's wrong, chicken? You had a good loss." Julie preened.

"No thanks to you," Kylie intervened. "And you made me put on 3lbs with all your rubbish about praying and reading the bible."

"Me? How could I make you put on 3lbs? It's what you stuff in your gob that makes you put on weight, and by the looks of you it wouldn't take much encouragement."

"Girls, girls, calm down. Look, Julie, have you anything you want to tell us, maybe get off your chest?" Selena asked.

"Me? No, why?" Said Julie, colouring faintly.

"So you don't consider it important, blabbing to everyone in the building about the club and what weight we all are, or that we might be upset?" questioned Selena.

"How mean can you be?" Cheryl said.

"You know how sensitive everyone is about their weight being broadcast."

"Do you need to make yourself so important at our expense?" from Selena.

"What have any of us done to you that would make you make fun of us?" cried Cheryl.

"Well, I hope you're happy – this is coming from Nearly Due Selena and Chunky Monkey Cheryl, we didn't get Kylie's nom de plume. As far as we're concerned you don't exist."

"Colossal Kylie," blurted Julie.

"WHAT?" roared Kylie. "Colossal Kylie? I'll Colossal you!" she said, taking a swipe at her but fortunately missing.

"Don't talk, text or email us. Go back to your other protégés who, incidentally, won't be here next week. They only came for a laugh, but remember they're laughing at you as much as us."

Julie, well and truly caught out, was sobbing, gulping and snuffling and desperately trying to make amends. She just hadn't thought what her actions had really done, but as far as the other three were concerned, that wasn't good enough. She wasn't sixteen. She was a grown woman who should have known better. She'd betrayed their trust and made them all look like fools, herself included.

The would-be-mentor sloped off with her tail well and truly between her legs, quite repentant for now.

Cheryl decided on the spur of the moment to ask the two remaining dieters for advice on her problem. She wasn't good with confidences and couldn't remember ever opening up to anyone outside of the family. Let's face it, she had never been in a situation anything like this and she was beside herself with worry.

"I wonder if I could ask for your opinion on something?" ventured Cheryl.

"Of course you can, not sure if we'll be any use, but fire away" said Selena.

"Yeah, go for it," said Kylie.

"Well, I know it's hard to believe, but I just got engaged and I'm getting married quite soon or at least I think I am, but I've just found out something huge and I'm worried sick," said the young bride-to-be.

"That's why you want to lose weight," Selena smiled. "Well, good for you."

"Yes, but no, but...it's more serious than that." Cheryl looked like she was about to burst into tears.

"If it's another woman, dump him," said Kylie. "Don't listen to any two-timing conniving jerk. If he does it now, he'll do it later."

"No, it's not another woman," she replied.

"You're not pregnant?" asked Selena.

"Well, that would be difficult. In fact it would be a miracle," she smiled weakly. "You can't get pregnant over the internet."

"Eh? Jesus, you're not a catalogue bride, are you?" queried Kylie.

"No, I've been friends with Doug for almost two years, he's in the States, by the way. At first we were just friends, good friends, but as time went by and the better we got to know one another we realised we were more than just good friends, we were soulmates. Last week he popped the question. Oh, it was so romantic, just perfect. He had the ring couriered to me and actually got down on one knee, it was perfect. When I said yes I had to open the box, and there was my ring. It is out of this world, fabulous in fact, but that's the problem."

"What, you don't like it?"

"Oh, I love it."

"Is it a fake?"

"No, definitely not. My problem started when I took it to Mr Cohen to be resized."

"Oh, I know him. Lovely man," ventured Selena.

"Shut up," said Kylie. "Let her get on with it."

"I'm just saying," Selena had to get the last word in.

"Shut up both of you and listen. I took it to Mr Cohen who refused to touch it."

"Dear God was it hot? Stolen?" said Kylie.

"It may well be, but that's irrelevant. It's what it's worth."

"What? The mean scumbag only spent a tenner?" mocked Kylie.

"A bit more than that," Cheryl laughed although that was the last thing she felt like.

"No, it wasn't worth ten quid. It's valued at over a quarter of a million pounds."

"Shit," said Kylie.

"And you've got a problem?" from Selena.

"Of course I've got a problem, but that's not all. He's always sending me gifts and I've had to take a few to Mr Cohen. According to him they're all real, not copies or fakes like I thought and worth thousands, in fact, hundreds of thousands."

"So what's your problem? I'd love to have it," laughed Selena.

"Well, where is he getting that kind of money from and why is he sending all this stuff to me? I don't know what to think," said poor Cheryl.

"Let me get this right," summed up Selena. "Your boyfriend, sorry, fiancé, whom you met online wants to marry you and has popped the question with a ring worth a quarter of a million dollars?"

"Pounds," corrected Cheryl.

"Sorry, pounds. And the other love tokens he's sent over the months add up to another hundred thousand pounds, is that about right?"

"Yes," ventured Cheryl.

"And you think you've got a problem?"

"Yes," replied Cheryl.

"Have you asked him about them?" said Selena.

"I can't."

"Eh, am I missing something here? Why could you not ask the man you think you are about to marry where he got almost half a million pounds, or dollars, to spend on knick knacks, for a woman he hasn't met yet and has only seen the top half of?"

"How did you know that?" asked Cheryl.

"It stands to reason, all the panic to lose weight. I told you, without a shadow of a doubt, you're the best-looking female in the class."

"That wouldn't be hard," sulked Kylie.

"So if he knew you weren't a size ten you wouldn't be here, correct?"

JULIE

Don't forget you are what you eat.
Okay, so I need to eat a skinny person!

Tonight was the weigh-in; she was as excited and nervous as a nun in a whore house. She was anxious for her girls and praying they'd all do well. By heavens, it wasn't for the lack of motivation. Every morning she'd sent little homilies to get them in the right frame of mind. Dieting was all about Positive Mental Attitude and she, Julie, certainly had mental attitude. Unfortunately though, it was unlike any other slimming guru's.

Then there were her new recruits. At least a dozen or so had promised to attend. The fact that at least half of them had less than five pounds to lose was not lost on Julie and she hoped these new members were coming for the right reason. She had heard a few giggles on her rounds about Chunky Monkey and Nearly Due Selena and she was beginning to feel a little edgy about her indiscretions over the past week. She hadn't meant to give away secrets, they had just sort of slipped out and she didn't trust that those in the know would keep the information to themselves. Most of them were in the same clique and not known for their kindness or diplomacy.

If she could keep them separate she might get away

with it, but with so many attending the class it would be like herding cats. Into the bargain she'd been asked to enrol the newbies to get the class started, which meant she had even less chance of keeping an eye on things and fending off unwanted questions.

She'd got through the weigh-in with no apparent disasters and two of the three had had fairly good losses. The big fish girl, Kylie, was a tad annoyed – making out that, she, Julie, was responsible for her putting on weight. Imagine thinking that she was to use the Bible and not the slimming bible, well, it could be confusing. But the fact that one hundred other people had not confused the two spoke volumes for Kylie's IQ.

To top off the evening and most likely because they wanted to ask for some tips and any little slimming gems, they were all retiring to the cafe for a skinny latte or two. This was just brilliant. It was just how she had envisaged her slimming class would be. Good results on the slimming front and then a little treat for the chosen few, the Dedicated Dieters: Julie's 'girls'.

She could see it now, and depending on how the conversation went, and if she felt she could really trust them (after all she couldn't abide gossip), she might let them into the company secret. She'd wait and see.

THEY TURNED ON HER, the three of them actually turned on her. How could they? After all she'd done for them. She'd set up gym sessions, arranged runs, not to mention depriving herself of real food as an inspiration to each of them. They had had the audacity to be angry with her. So she'd maybe let the cat out of the bag a couple of times, but she wasn't saying anything that wasn't true. They were all three of them overweight. She supposed that the rest of the staff maybe shouldn't know what they weighed and maybe she shouldn't have disclosed the nicknames she'd given them, but to turn on her with such viciousness? She couldn't believe it! Well, no secret for them, not that it would affect Kylie, but the other two would suffer. She didn't know if she would accept their apologies, only down on bended knees would do.

Kylie

If you can't tell a spoon from a ladle, you're fat!

Bouncing cheerfully into work, she expected balloons and streamers, and all her workmates wishing her many happy returns and Happy Birthday. Were they all going to jump out shouting 'Surprise!' at her? It seemed not, no-one even called out good morning, never mind Happy Birthday.

What was going on? Birthdays were always made special. Everyone was made a fuss of, so what was happening, or more to the point, not happening?

She was being stupid; of course, they would be playing a prank on her and pretending they hadn't remembered. Okay, she could play along with this. So, humming away to herself, and to everyone's surprise, she got on with her work. All the while daydreaming about the surprise she was sure they were all planning to spring on her.

She was so lost in her thoughts she failed to notice how quiet it had become. Oh my God, it was break time. Psyching herself up to look surprised, she pushed open the canteen door. She was met with nothing but the crashing sound of silence. This was taking a joke too far. Nobody, not even Mandy, her BFF, had wished her Happy Birthday or produced as much as a French Fancy. As for her boyfriend, some boyfriend, not even a text. They couldn't all have forgotten, surely? They wouldn't forget her birthday. After all, she was probably one of the most popular workers, if not the most popular. She knew they all loved her; they were always saying stuff like the place wasn't the same since she'd started work there. They couldn't understand how she still worked there, and loads more stuff. Everybody liked Kylie, but no-one more than Kylie herself.

She couldn't believe that all her friends and workmates, especially Mandy and Jason, could treat her this way. There had to be an explanation. She knew they had been into town recently to buy her birthday present. Hadn't she brought cakes in for everyone without being prompted and only eaten a couple? She had been sweetness and light all week. So what was going on?

Of course, how could she be so stupid? There was obviously a huge surprise party planned for this evening. She'd really have to act surprised and stunned. Such a pity she couldn't wear 'The Dress'.

Kylie

I am in shape – round is a shape.

Somewhat placated, she made her way back to work only to be summoned to Human Resources. She couldn't be getting a present from the management, could she? It wasn't usual, but if anyone deserved it, Kylie reckoned she did. Wow, that would certainly be something to swank about. A present from management or maybe it was a presentation. Best employee or Employee of the Month? She sped off as fast as she could, which wasn't fast, given her bulk.

It looked very official for a birthday bash. There was Mr Tompkins, HR Director, skinny Edith, his P.A. and Bill the foreman, who looked like the cat who'd gotten the cream. She knew he liked her, but this was getting a bit pervy. Maybe she'd have to get their Sean to have a word.

Oh, it was a presentation alright, her being presented with a verbal warning - a verbal warning? The bloody cheek of it, absolutely bloody cheek. If it wasn't her birthday she would tell human resources to stick their job where the sun don't shine, but no, she'd keep calm, after all she had tonight to look forward to. Imagine them having the nerve to say she was not up to standard. Her! She, Kylie Harper was not up to the job? She was gutting fucking fish. Who couldn't be up to the job?

Well, obviously her she mused, and they were extending her probation period by another month. Miserable bastards, they just didn't want to pay her the full rate. That was it, nothing to do with her being up to the job or not. If she was on full rate, she'd bankrupt them. What a birthday this was turning out to be. Tonight had better be extra special.

She declined an offer to go out for a family meal, she knew it was just a ploy to get her to the party, but no way was she arriving with her parents. How cool would that look? So she was ready and waiting for 'the call'. She had, in fact, been ready since just after five, knowing how the gang could party. They were cutting it a bit fine though, it was almost eight o'clock and not a cheep from anyone. What the devil were they all playing at? She texted and texted everyone she knew and not one single reply. What was the point in them all keeping a secret if they kept it from her?

The clock struck midnight, her birthday was officially over. What a fucking disaster. She was absolutely gobsmacked. Where was everybody? Even Mum and Dad were still out. She knew they were all at a surprise party somewhere in town and the surprise was that they had forgotten to tell her. She knew, she absolutely knew they were all partying somewhere without her. A very confused Kylie climbed into bed and lay staring at 'The Dress'. Just wait till they all see me in this, she thought. I'll knock them dead, she vowed as she finished off the last of the birthday cake.

Well, bugger them, no way would she share it after the night she had just had. The fact she had had no-one to share it with seemed lost on her.

JULIE

Keep calm, the hunger will pass.

She was so upset she hardly slept that night. To help pass the time, three a.m. saw her trawling the internet in an effort to find out more about this hostile take-over. She had actually compiled quite a dossier on Mr Douglas Winthrop III and his company, DW3 Corporation. It was amazing how much information was out there; it was just a case of sifting through every piece of minutiae and she was nothing if not persistent.

It seemed that this mystery man had begun trading almost ten years ago and had been hailed as a financial genius, the kid with the Midas touch. He could do no wrong; every investment reaped huge benefits and he was featured in the Wall Street Journal and Time magazine as the new and youngest whiz kid on the block. He couldn't spend the money as fast as he was earning it. And boy, he tried. He lived the life of the original rich kid through the media. Everything he did was in the glare of publicity. Then disaster had struck: the double dip recession and millions wiped off the Stock Exchange. As quickly as he rose to fame, he fell. Overnight he lost almost everything.

The yacht was first to go, then the Ferrari. The stunning models didn't hang around for long and most of his so-called friends also disappeared. The party was over. But for him it was just another challenge. He'd done it once, he sure as hell could do it again, but very differently this time and he'd make sure he kept it this time.

He retreated from public life and conducted all his business from his penthouse, the one asset that was non-negotiable, nothing would make him sell or move from there. Within five years he had risen back to the top, but without the publicity or notoriety. A combination of smoke and mirrors allowed Mr Douglas Winthrop III to remain anonymous. His company still operated from the flashy offices on Wall Street and employed flash brokers with huge expense accounts. This was a measure of success in his business. But few employees knew who they worked for, and even fewer had ever met him. He lived his life online.

Sifting through the hundreds of companies bought and sold through DW3 Corp. Julie came across a small pharmaceutical company in Wyoming which had been bought by the corporation, but for some reason had been allowed to continue business as usual. They had been in the grip of the corporation for almost three years. This in itself was unusual. The big boys operated the same modus operandi in every deal. The companies were broken up into divisions and sold. Never did a company remain intact, and this small outfit seemed to be actually losing them money. There had to be a catch or a reason.

Then she found it! The reason was that this small Mom and Pop laboratory in the back of beyond had found the Elixir of Life. Well, not quite, but definitely the second best thing. The diet industry in the US was worth five billion dollars a year and the company who could come up with the real McCoy: finding the product that really would make a person thin was worth hundreds of millions of dollars. DW3 Corporation owned the pharmaceutical company that had done just that and that was the reason they had not been sold.

Julie wasn't interested in saving her company from the take-over; she wasn't interested in the Mom and Pop Company and its employees when this went public. She had only one goal and that was to get the product and GET THIN then all her worries would be behind her.

Cheryl

Brain cells come and brain cells go.
But fat cells go on forever.

Quarter of a million pounds, quarter of a million? It kept going round and round in her head. Who the devil spent that on a ring? Who could spend that amount of money on a ring? My God, they'd still be paying it up when they were in their 80's. Quarter of a million? What was she going to do? She had no problem following her diet, she was too sick to her stomach to eat. What about the other pieces? She had never for one moment thought they were genuine. Everybody nowadays bought copies. They were damned good ones, but copies all the same. Well, not according to Mr Cohen, he reckoned the watch was worth a couple of grand and the Cartier bracelet about the same.

He hadn't seen the Tiffany necklace, not the common one everyone had, but a stunning, gold-coloured piece. And the fabulous Bulgari ring, Michael Kors earrings and, if what he said was correct, she shuddered to think what the diamond studded Rolex was worth. She had at least another twenty grand in gifts.

In her heart she had always known it to be too good to be true. She could never attract someone like Doug, not in real life. In cyber space maybe, but not in reality. But why was he showering her with gifts? What reason would he have for sending all these thousands of pounds, hundreds of thousands of pounds to her? Why? What was his plan? Was he a bank robber? No, that didn't make sense. Had he ordered all this stuff online and given a false address? Jesus, was the FBI going to appear at her home and arrest her?

She was distraught, she didn't know what to think, but one thing for sure – she had to get rid of all this stuff, but how and where? And how was she going to get rid of Doug? Could she dump him? What else could she do?

There was no way she could be involved in this scam, whatever it was.

Kylie

I am a nutritional overachiever.

"Hi Selena, it's Kylie from the slimming club. How are things?"

"Oh! Hi Kylie, I'm fine, struggling a bit, what about you?"

"I'm okay, but guess what I've just done?"

"I'm not sure I want to know."

"Don't worry, it's nothing illegal. I've just made an appointment with a hypnotherapist for Tuesday evening. He says he can hypnotise me into hating chocolate. It's a bit expensive, but think what I'll save on sweets."

"I'm not so sure. A girl who works in here went to a hypnotist, she lost a bit of weight, but every time someone mentioned chicken, she had to cross the road."

"I remember seeing her, she used to squawk and pretend to flap her wings, it was hysterical."

"Yes, but not in the middle of the high street. You be careful."

"I'm still going, I've got to do something. Speak to you later, bye."

Climbing the stairs to the hypnotist's clinic, Kylie couldn't get the chicken scenario out of her head. What if she suddenly started squawking or tried to perch on a chair or, God forbid, tried to lay an egg? No, maybe this wasn't such a good idea. Maybe she'd just deal with the chocolate cravings another way.

But just as Kylie was about to go back down the stairs, the receptionist called her name. Shit, should she run? That was a bit childish. Pretend she wasn't Kylie? No, she'd listen to what the therapist had to say and then make up her mind.

Before she knew it she was on her way back down the stairs and on to the pavement. "Hey, what the devil happened there?" she muttered to herself. Was that all there was to it? Had she been relieved of her chocolate cravings? It all seemed a bit suspect. She remembered nothing about the consultation but she had been relieved of £100 and what was worse she could murder a Mars bar. Maybe it took time to kick in?

CHERYL

I just ran my first marathon – just joking –
I'm on my third cupcake!

Thankfully Cheryl hadn't spoken to Doug for a couple of nights, just a few e-mails and texts had passed between them. He had told her weeks ago that he had to attend a course somewhere, she couldn't for the life of her remember where, and he would be out of town for two or three nights. She was so relieved. For one thing, she was hopeless at lying and she was fairly sure he would be able to tell right away that there was something up, and there sure was something up.

Terrified wandering around town with all these valuables, Cheryl had no choice; she needed to know if Mr Cohen's estimate was correct. So, venturing into one of the large stores in town she produced the Bulgari ring to be valued. Immediately the assistant called the manager. God, was she going to get arrested? The damned stuff was stolen! Could she make a bolt for it? Unfortunately she wasn't built for sprinting. What would she do with the rest of her 'gifts'? The police were sure to search her. Damn. Damn. Damn. How could she have ever believed the lying two-faced rat?

Oops, maybe she'd been a bit hasty. The terribly posh manager had come up with a similar value to Mr Cohen, so there was no question of the ring being fake and he gave no indication that it was on some hot list from Interpol or whoever issued hot lists. He'd pee his shiny grey pants if he got a butchers at her engagement ring. She laughed, even though she wasn't feeling the slightest bit humorous.

She made her way back to Mr Cohen with the rest of Doug's gifts, on the pretext of getting an insurance valuation. He was delighted to see her and she felt a little guilty at using him in this way, but the old man raved over her pieces, was ecstatic over the craftsmanship of her acquisitions and hammered a nail into her heart with every piece he valued.

Conservatively, including her engagement ring, her haul stood at around three hundred and ten thousand pounds. She felt sick.

Why, she asked herself? Why would anyone give her gifts worth this astronomical sum? There was nothing about this that made any sense. She could have sold them immediately, the moment she had received them, and pocketed the money. There would have been nothing Doug could do to retrieve it; she could have given the things away. Why?

How could she have spent all this time getting to know a person, only to be absolutely and utterly fooled by him? It didn't seem possible. She wasn't some gullible, young virgin. Lonely, maybe, but she was no mug. She would have staked her life that there was little or nothing she didn't know about him. Surely if he was a criminal on this scale she would have detected something?

He had told her about his company failing and how he was left with virtually nothing. She knew that he had started up again and was doing alright. But nothing about him being some kind of international jewel thief. It was very clever of him to send his ill-gotten gains by Royal Mail. What unsuspecting postie would believe he was delivering a fifty thousand pound watch that didn't even need signed for? Or the unique Tiffany necklace that was worth at least ten thousand. The engagement ring had come by FedEx, but even that had been undervalued. Simply stating birthday gift and zero value which she thought was to avoid her suspicions and spoil the surprise. Was this a double bluff? A parcel was unlikely to be stolen in transit if marked no value and she couldn't prove the goods had come to her by legitimate means. What the devil was she going to do? How could she dispose of them? The girls were of no real help, but then what could she expect? How many times in your life are you presented with someone asking you how to dispose of three hundred thousand pounds worth of jewellery? Not very often.

Dear God, that damned stupid woman was still bombarding her with bloody emails. She was one thing Cheryl would sort out. Julie was first on her agenda when she got to work; enough was enough. Cheryl certainly didn't need anyone's motivation or intervention right now. Her diet had certainly fallen by the wayside but she was so worried and upset that for once in her life she wasn't comfort-eating.

She was going to have to come up with something fast. Doug was back today and would be online this evening. She couldn't feign an illness, she'd already done that the two days before he left on his trip.

Could she risk just asking him – Selena's solution? No way, forewarned is forearmed and if he thought it was business as usual it would give her a bit more wriggle room to come up with a plan. She couldn't think of any feasible explanation for his ability to buy all these extravagant gifts.

SELENA

There's only one thing that keeps me off my diet... food!

Selena was beyond surprised that she'd lost any weight this week as her head was all over the place. She'd found it difficult to follow diets in the past, but that was usually through boredom after a while, not in the first few weeks. She was constantly starving. Really hungry, and no matter what she consumed, she couldn't rid herself of the hunger pangs. With so much at stake, she had to master this, she had no alternative, but it was so difficult.

The bars and shakes were out of the question, she simply couldn't survive on that regime. Vegetables, she would eat only vegetables, in fact, what about the Cabbage Soup diet? She'd tried it many years ago and had lost loads of weight, but like most of these faddy plans, when you stop, the weight piles on with a vengeance. But she only needed to stay slim for a specific period of time.

That night she made her first batch of soup. The ethos behind this plan was that the dieter would make soup using specific ingredients and on a daily basis it would be topped up so that by Friday it resembled primeval sludge, but the celebs said it worked.

The smell in the house was unbearable, but being the good husband he was, Winston bore it. Unfortunately

Selena had forgotten the major drawback to this soup. Flatulence! OMG, it was like pure methane and she was terrified to go near a naked flame, she would surely blow up. It was bad enough for Winston, but her work colleagues were not so forgiving or kind.

It started with the odd sniff and comments about the drains being a bit off. By Wednesday someone had called 'a man' in. The man could find nothing wrong with the plumbing, having dug up two thirds of the flooring and pronouncing that it was human plumbing that was to blame. Everyone looked at Selena who protested vehemently, so much so that she let off a little one and almost gassed the whole department. Early bath and all the office windows open; time for a re-think.

Next was the juicer. According to the blurb on the telly and the man in neon lycra, you just throw everything into this machine and hey presto, drink the delicious smoothie and you were guaranteed to shed pounds and pounds.

Standing in the kitchen, not dressed in puce lycra, Selena filled the new juicer which had cost a mere £199 and filled it to the brim with exotic fruits (£15) and produced her first trickle. Filling the machine to the top again (£12) there was another trickle. She'd be bankrupt at this rate. The trickles tasted fabulous but were gone in one gulp. Unfortunately, delicious as they might be, the liquid had the same effect on Selena's poor intestines as the cabbage soup, and the acid produced by all these fruits had her doubled in two for most of the day, making her workmates almost green but not with envy. She was at her wit's end.

How were the others managing? Lord, what a bunch of misfits they were, thought Selena. This neurotic woman, with delusions of grandeur, had taken it on herself to lead the troops to the land of semi-skimmed milk and sugar-free honey. Who considered emailing absolute rubbish to 'her girlies' to be the height of motivation, which she hoped would result in amazing weight loss? She advocated the most absurd methods and would swallow anything so long as it had been endorsed by some half-wit celebrity. How daft did Julie think they were? Or more to the point, how daft did she think Selena was?

Then there was 'the fiancée', a lump of a girl who could, with a little work and the loss of a couple of stones, be absolutely stunning. But she had no self-confidence whatsoever and chose to spend her time closeted in the dark, hour after hour, online with some guy who, it seemed, had popped the question. He could be anybody, a mass murderer, a serial killer or even a bigamist. Mind you, with three hundred thousand in her bottom drawer, who gave a shit? Selena had to admit the whole thing was bizarre.

The third member of their little group was the most self-deluded, over-indulged, overweight, precocious young woman Selena had ever encountered. There were obviously no mirrors in Kylie's home. Because how Kylie thought she looked bore no resemblance to how Kylie actually looked. Despite this, the girl was super confident and couldn't contemplate for one minute that she was anything less than perfect.

From the few tit-bits they had gleaned from her, Selena had no idea how the girl had managed to keep her job. Not that she was bothered in the slightest if she did or not. Her employment status seemed to hinge on her BFF Mandy and her boyfriend Jason, who appeared to be more enamoured with Mandy than with our heroine. As long as they both worked in the fish factory, then so would Kylie.

Selena was desperately trying to remain positive but knew that it was very unlikely that she would succeed, either with the group or the slimming club. The reality was that to qualify for her IVF treatment her target weight was way beyond the realms of possibility. Sadly, she had probably left it too late. The traditional weight loss programmes were too slow for her. She needed drastic measures and she needed them now.

Maybe Julie wasn't so daft after all? Maybe Selena would have to go down that route? She would certainly give it some thought; maybe talk it over with Cheryl when she got back from lunch. OMG, another three emails from Julie all winging their way to the trashcan.

KYLIE

*If fatty means 'full of fat' shouldn't skinny
mean 'full of skin'?*

It was a week since her awful birthday and things
had got progressively worse. Mandy and Jason, it
turned out, had been off all weekend, visiting some
old school friend. The fact that they had grown up
in different towns and were three years apart in age
struck her as a bit suspect, but they were so apologetic,
and were positive that one of the others had arranged
a celebration. As for the special birthday present, a tin
of toffees that looked suspiciously like the ones left
over from the Secret Santa draw. It certainly wouldn't
have taken long in town to make that purchase.

She was beginning to have doubts about them. She
knew they were good mates, but they were spending
just a little too much time together.

There was no way Mandy would betray Kylie, it
just wasn't done. She knew that the two of them had
had a bit of a thing before Kylie caught his eye, or
grabbed him by the proverbial, but that didn't count.
Mandy was her BFF and Jason was 'her Jason'. There
was no more to be said.

All this stress was playing havoc with her diet.
She'd hopped on to the new scales this morning to find
they were out of sync too. According to them she'd

111

gained 4lbs. Not possible, she had virtually starved herself all week. She knew she'd had a bit too much birthday cake, but she'd made up for that by running to catch the bus this morning. She'd have to run to work the rest of this week and go to the gym after she finished. Yep! That's what she'd do, she still had a few weeks to get the pounds off, she could do it, and after all, she had a will of iron.

Adding a few more marshmallows to the steaming mug of hot chocolate, she settled down for an evening with the television. She had to build her strength up for her ordeal tomorrow. Maybe a choccy biccy to dunk, just the one?

Shit! She was going to be late again. Why the devil had her mum let her sleep in? No time to run to work, she'd have to catch the bus. Grabbing a packet of crisps and a couple of chocolate biscuits for breakfast, off she hurried. No way was she letting Pervy Bill catch her clocking-in late. She made it with seconds to spare and she was sure he looked miffed as he marched away from the clocking-in station. He definitely had a thing for her.

By tea break she was starving. She could have easily eaten a raw fish she was so famished. Racing up to the canteen and pushing her way right to the front of the queue, she ordered two bacon butties and a huge mug of tea. She was in no mood for namby pamby grub. She was a working girl and she needed her strength, she'd cut back on lunch and tea, she argued with herself.

The idiots from packing were up to their usual stupid antics. Calling out to her, making remarks about all the weight she'd lost and glad to see she was keeping up with her eating plan, cheeky sods. Maybe she was losing inches but not pounds? That did happen, she'd read it in a magazine and if it wasn't true they couldn't print it, could they? Maybe she hadn't put on weight, she was probably building muscle and everyone knew muscle weighed more than fat. Well, it could be so. She'd try the dress on tonight.

Lunchtime saw her running, a fast walk was nearer the mark, to the park, which was all of approximately one hundred metres from work. "Goodness, this exercise lark didn't half work up an appetite," she mumbled to herself. She was only enduring it, having arranged to meet Jason at half past and as usual she was behind time.

Having brought him a selection of sandwiches and tit-bits for lunch, she was somewhat disappointed to see Mandy jogging towards her. Much as she loved Mandy, and Jason certainly didn't seem to mind her joining them, Kylie wanted some alone time with him and it never happened. What Mandy needed was a boyfriend of her own.

"Hi," called Mandy, "on your own?"

"Waiting for Jason," replied Kylie. "We're having lunch together."

"That's strange" said Mandy, jogging on the spot. "I've just passed him on the way back from the canteen."

"No, you must be mistaken. We're having lunch together. I've got all his favourite things."

"Well, he was certainly on his way back to work. Check your phone, maybe he's sent you a message?" said Mandy, still jogging. "Look I've got to go, don't want to be late. You know what that old fart is like, see ya," and off her BFF jogged.

No message from Jason, in fact no messages from anyone. Kylie was not best pleased and what about all this food? Well she couldn't let it go to waste.

JULIE

Why can't mosquitos suck fat instead of blood?

Julie was like a half-shut knife for most of the morning and despite several emails to her girlies, she'd had no replies. She knew they were still cross with her, but when they found out what she'd discovered all would be well, or at least she hoped it would.

She had puzzled all night and in fact had almost taken a duvet day today, but had decided against it. After all, the sooner she faced everyone, the better. Surely, with the assistance of Selena and Cheryl, the three of them could come up with a way of getting this wonder drug, or whatever it was.

She bumped slap-bang into Selena in the lift and fortunately there were no other occupants.

"Morning, Selena," she ventured. "How are you this morning?"

"No better for seeing you," retorted Selena. "I told you last night, I don't want to hear another word from you and you shouldn't be emailing. I've had three already this morning."

"I know! I know, but I've discovered something, Selena, something absolutely incredible, but I need help."

"Oh, you need help right enough, and never mind what you've discovered. We discovered what a low-life you really are to our cost last night," replied Selena exiting the lift.

"Wait, wait, Selena!" but the lift doors had already closed and Julie was halfway to the next floor.

Still a little flustered by her encounter, who was waiting on the next floor but Cheryl? As the doors opened and Cheryl came face to face with her quarry, she barged in.

"Just the person I was looking for," snarled Cheryl. "I cannot believe what a snake in the grass you turned out to be. Everyone knows what a gossip and scandalmonger you are, but pretending to be our friend and mentor when all the time it was just to gain popularity. I've decided I'm going to HR to make an official complaint and if I can persuade anyone else to do the same, I will. Never have I come across such a nasty piece of work. I'm not surprised your husband divorced you and I pity your boys."

By now there were a few other occupants in the lift who were cheering Cheryl on.

"Fight, fight," was being chanted and nearly everyone on the third floor was being royally entertained.

Cheryl could have died of mortification. The only way she got through her days at work was to keep such a low profile that many of her colleagues thought she was a visitor. There was no hiding place today.

Julie, on the other hand, was well known and more than one of the audience had been the subject of Julie's tittle tattle over the years. Despite wanting to slink away, Julie stood her ground, pulling Cheryl into the lift, hoping for a little privacy. No chance, half the department squeezed into the confined space, baying for blood. Anybody's, but preferably Julie's.

SELENA

I have a condition that stops me from dieting - hunger

The news of Cheryl and Julie's fracas went round the building like wildfire and by the time Selena was the recipient of the news, one or the other had been carted off on a stretcher to A&E. No matter how angry Selena was, she wouldn't have wanted any harm to come to the two protagonists. Firing off a quick email to both parties to ascertain they were both alive and kicking, and hopefully not the shit out of each other, she was relieved to get replies that all was well and they had in fact made up.

Selena was astounded to discover that Cheryl had arranged to meet with the lunatic for coffee after work and was all for washing her hands of the pair of them. But curiosity was getting the better of her and, despite her better judgement, she agreed to consider Cheryl's request to come along and hear what Julie had to say. She wondered what monumental piece of garbage Julie would be imparting.

Selena really wasn't in the mood for extracurricular activities. She had been feeling out of sorts all day and really wanted to go straight home and put her feet up. However, in order to delay the consumption of another plate of inedible porridge-like substance, she made her way to the coffee shop.

Both women were already ensconced in a booth with steaming cups of latte on Selena's arrival. Making no bones about her reasons for coming, Selena bounced herself down on the sofa, declining the offer of a drink.

"Okay, what's the monumentally incredible piece of news you have that will change our lives?" Selena demanded.

"Well..." drawled Julie.

"Look, if this is rubbish I'm out of here," snapped Cheryl. "No more dramatics. Spit it out."

"Okay, okay. I'll do my best to keep it short," said Julie. "But you have to bear with me."

"No! We don't," said the two in unison. "Just get on with it."

"Sure you won't have a coffee before I start?" Julie queried.

"GET ON WITH IT," from Selena.

"Well, as I was saying, I have discovered something that will change our lives."

"You're not reinventing the wheel are you?"

"Better than that," said Julie. "I have come across the very latest and the most successful slimming drug ever."

Both of her companions got up to go.

"I knew it would be rubbish," snapped Selena. "What a waste of time."

"Bloody hell, Julie! How pathetic are you?"

"Listen, both of you. This is no stupid celebrity thing, this is the real McCoy. This is the brainchild of a chemist in Wyoming and a division of the company about to buy ours out."

"What did you say? Selena demanded.

"It's the brain child of a chemist..."

"Not that bit you idiot, the bit about our company being bought out."

"Oh, yes. That's almost a done deal."

Selena burst into tears. "You're joking? We're not really going to be taken over?" she snuffled.

"Yes, we are and it was because of the takeover that I found this information," Julie smirked.

"Look, what the hell do you think we can do to stop a takeover? Don't be bloody stupid," said Cheryl, still on her feet ready to go.

"Sit down and let me explain. Trust me it will all come clear," pleaded Julie.

"TRUST YOU? You've got to be joking. Whatever you've got to say I'm sure it's very interesting, but I've got a hell of a night in front of me and I could be doing without all this palaver."

"Five minutes, that's all it'll take," Julie pleaded. "Just five minutes."

"I was so upset over what had happened that I couldn't sleep and ended up on my laptop till the wee small hours. At first I was just googling anything and everything when I stumbled across the company involved in the takeover."

"And...?"

"Well, I thought I would try to find out as much

as I could about them. Maybe we won't all lose our jobs. Maybe they're a better outfit than the one we work for at the moment. Well, I dug and I dug and came up with all sorts of random stuff on them. Who they were and how long they'd been in business. You know, all the usual stuff. It seems the company is run by some mysterious entrepreneur who keeps in the shadows, never really appears in public and most of his employees don't even know him."

"So?"

"Well, I do and so do you, Selena."

"Oh, yeah, I know millions of billionaires, can't get up my path for them."

"You do, you met him last year. The great big Texan guy, you couldn't forget him," smiled Julie.

"Look," and she handed over the photograph to Selena. "God, how could you forget him? There was some delegation or something and he was with them. Youngish guy, quiet. Well, he's Douglas Winthrop III and he's the guy who's taking over this company. And his corporation own the newest drug coming on to the market which will guarantee no more obesity. And we have to get to him."

"That's easy" whispered Cheryl. "I'll ask him tonight."

"WHAT?"

REVELATIONS

You're not fat – come on, chin up,
and the other one,
and the other one.

"WHAT?" both ladies cried out in unison. "What do you mean you'll speak to him tonight?"

"She's delirious," said Julie. "Probably needs something to eat. Sugar levels, yeah, her sugar level's down."

"Shut up, you idiot. The last thing I need is something to eat," snapped Cheryl. "I'm on a diet or had you forgotten?"

"Listen girl, if we can get these pills you'll never have to go on another diet in your life, I promise you," said Julie. "And if you know him, we're home and dry."

"Never mind the sodding pills. How do you know this guy, Cheryl?" Selena questioned.

"He's my fiancé," groaned Cheryl. "That guy in the picture is Doug, my fiancé. The guy I've been dating online for almost two years. The guy who got down on one knee and proposed. The guy I thought I knew inside out. The one person I could trust, that I had no secrets from and he had none from me, well that's rich."

"Yes, and how," chipped in Selena.

"Okay, so he didn't tell you he had a revolutionary slimming programme. Maybe he wanted to test it further?" cajoled Julie.

"A Fucking Slimming Programme? Are you as fucking stupid as you look?" snarled Cheryl. "Oh, he kept a bit more than a slimming pill from me. Try a few billion dollars and his whole life."

"What am I going to do?" Cheryl beseeched Selena. "What am I going to do?"

"Just ask him outright, get a couple of dozen. That should do for starters," hustled Julie "Or do either of you want some? In that case, make it four dozen."

"Is she still on about bloody slimming pills?" asked Cheryl "Tell her, Selena, tell her or so help me, I'll swing for her."

"Calm down, Cheryl, calm down. My God, this is like something out of Pretty Woman."

"What are you saying? That I'm a bloody prozzy?" the bride-to-be answered back. "Mind you, if I take all this," pulling piece after piece of jewellery out of her bag. "I might as well be one. At least I wasn't cheap."

"Hey, where did this all come from? It's fabulous."

"Jesus, Cheryl, put that away. Don't pull it out in here, you'll get mugged," protested Selena.

"I already have been," said the despondent Cheryl.

"Now, don't you do anything rash," said Julie, trying on rings and bracelets. "Are these actually for real?" she gasped in admiration.

"Oh, they're for real, almost four hundred thousand pounds real. Enough to buy my own pharmaceutical company. What do you say to that, Julie? Will I make my own miracle slimming cure?"

"Do you think you could?" said Julie, all wide eyes.

"No, she doesn't, you twat." said Selena. Turning to Cheryl, "What are you going to do, or more to the point, what will you say to him?"

"I don't know, I don't think I ever want to speak to him again," said Cheryl, huge crystal tears running down her cheeks. "I don't think I could ever trust a word he says. Maybe this was all just a joke to him. Let's face it, I'm not much of a catch, am I?"

"Not really," said Julie ducking as Selena side-swiped her off the sofa.

"Of course you are, maybe he wanted to get to know you without the money getting in the way? Let's face it, you've just found out about it and already it's causing problems."

"Causing problems? It's doing more than cause problems. We're through, finished." Cheryl replied. "It's not the money that's causing the problems, it's the fact I didn't know about it. How different is his life from the person I thought he was?

"When he told me he'd seen a new film, I presumed he'd gone out with friends to a multiplex, not to a private viewing in his own home theatre. When he goes bowling, it's down to the basement where he has his own alley, not as I thought, smelly shoes and the lane booked for an hour. It's over," sobbed Cheryl.

"Has he really got a private cinema and bowling alley?" queried Julie.

"For goodness sake!" said an exasperated Selena. "How the hell would she know that? She's only saying."

"Look, Cheryl, like Julie said, don't go burning your boats, there could be a perfectly reasonable explanation although I can't think of one for the moment, but there could be."

"Yes, just think how terrible it would be to have more money than you could spend in three lifetimes. Limousines, private jets and cruising in the Caribbean and that's just for starters. Yes, it would be absolutely awful. Hey, give him my email if you don't want him," laughed Julie

"It's not funny, you halfwit."

"Well, I've had worse problems. Why on earth would you dump a guy because he's loaded? And let's face it, you're not likely to get many other chances," quipped Julie.

"Don't be so nasty," interrupted Selena. "But you know, Julie says it like it is, and this time she's right. Why would you dump him because he's rich? In fact, why would you dump him at all? He's fit, really fit."

Cheryl had had enough; she didn't seem to be able to get through to them how desolate and betrayed she felt, she had to go. She had to deal with this on her own.

KYLIE

We all have one skinny friend,
who eats twice what a fat person does.

Guaranteed to lose 20lbs in one week? No damned wonder a person could lose 20lbs, the taste was absolutely disgusting – she had never tasted anything so vile. Oh! She was going to throw up, she had to have something to take away this dreadful taste. Spying the biscuit barrel, she grabbed a handful and stuffed them into her mouth, still the taste persisted. She was beginning to despair, time was marching on and the others in the club were doing okay. Selena had lost almost a stone, but half of that was water, so she'd told her. Maybe Kylie could have a huge long wee and lose a few pounds; it was worth a try.

Cheryl was also much thinner, but looked terrible. Stupid mare was pining for the Yank, mused Kylie. Imagine dumping him after she found out his little secret. Well, not exactly a little secret, three or four billion secrets. For some reason Cheryl had gotten it into her head she wasn't good enough for him. Whatever! What was so special about the guy anyway, well, apart from his money? He must be a bit of a div. C'mon, if he couldn't find anyone in real life with all that dosh there had to be something seriously wrong.

Kylie found this hilarious. Given half a chance she would. No, she wouldn't, she had her Jason.

What about the mad woman? She had really shifted the weight; she was like a different person. Still sending those bloody stupid emails, but they went straight into Kylie's junk mail. She didn't even open them and she certainly hadn't opened the 'Bible', not the Jesus one, since the first weigh-in. She was starting to panic, there was no way she could get into the dress and things were getting desperate. Despite that, there was no way she could endure the Seaweed and Nettle diet, it was bad, really bad.

What was she going to do? She had already been to a seamstress to see if the dress could be let out. Never again would she give that woman a stitch to sew. Telling her to take it back and get a refund. Get a refund, on the most wonderful creation ever seen? The dress that was going to change her life, the dress that would make her look at least three stones thinner, the dress that would make Jason see her as she really was, beautiful, desirable and better looking than Mandy. The dress that would make him propose. Get a refund? No chance! She would get into it and she would be the belle of the ball.

Cheryl

My food preference is often.

She'd dashed off an email to Human Resources last night, informing them that she was taking a couple of weeks leave (unpaid if necessary) to sort out a family problem. Well, that was true. And never having taken time off in the past, she saw no reason why it should be a problem. Not that it mattered if it was, according to what Julie had implied last night none of them would have a job in the next couple of weeks anyway. Mr Douglas Winthrop the third could simply deduct it from her next pay cheque or redundancy pay. Whatever!

She had a thumping headache, and a stiff neck, having slept on the sofa. Well, passed out was more like it. The empty bottles could testify to that. She'd lost count of the number of emails, texts, Facebook and Twitter messages from her ex-fiancé, who seemed somewhat put out that she, a mere female, had dumped him. It appeared he could think of no reason for her sudden change of mind while she could think of at least three billion. Thank God she had kept the engagement to herself. How humiliating would that have been? Let's face it, it would simply reinforce the opinion most of her colleagues had of her anyway. Well, they could think what they liked, but the reality was, few would even notice she wasn't there.

Checking the time, she had just over an hour to get packed. Her taxi was booked for 11a.m. The cheap ticket to Malaga had seemed a fantastic idea last night. Well, she rationalised to herself, if she was going to be miserable she may as well be miserable in the sun. Anyway, she hadn't seen her younger sister for months, not since Laura had landed herself a job for the season in sunny Spain.

Doug was shattered at the news. The text had just said "Finished – change of heart – good luck for the future. C."

He read and reread the message, each time hoping it was a mistake. He couldn't believe it. Why? What had he done? Was there someone else? Probably, wasn't there usually? He had vowed years ago he would never get serious about a woman again, he'd been dumped too many times and then he'd met Cheryl. Right from the start they had hit it off, they had got on fantastically. They liked the same things, were into the same stuff and over the months and years had shared all their secrets, they were great friends. He thought he knew everything about her when he had finally plucked up the courage to propose and when she said yes, he was over the moon.

It was a shame that because of business commitments, he couldn't be in the UK for a few weeks yet and maybe he should have waited, but once he had decided, he was desperate to seal the deal. He loved her and wanted everyone to know.

Sure, he'd sent her a few nice pieces, trinkets really, and she seemed to like and appreciate them. And her reaction when she saw the engagement ring he'd picked for her, well, it really blew him away. Not for a minute had he ever thought she was a golddigger.

"You look amazing," said her sister, hugging her, "absolutely amazing. Certainly not like the washed-out, lovelorn poor soul I was expecting. To tell you the truth, I was sure you'd be comfort-eating and be even bigger than the last time I saw you. I can't get over it, you've lost tons of weight. So what's the story then?"

"Hell of a way to go on a diet," replied Cheryl. "Honestly, I don't really want to talk about it just now. I need to get some food, I've not really eaten for... well for ages."

"No way, you're not getting off that easily. I need to hear all the gory details."

"No gory details, just a sad pathetic mug who should have known better," said a very-sorry-for-herself Cheryl.

"Okay, food, story then bed. Deal?" asked Laura. "After that, no more questions, just two weeks of soaking up the sun and repairing your poor heart."

Her younger sister dished up a steaming plate of pasta, together with loads of cheap Spanish plonk (not the best, but it certainly hit the mark), and relaxing in the warm Spanish air, Cheryl enlightened her sister about her recent adventures.

"My God, only you could get into this mess!" laughed the young girl. "But why have you finished with him? Why haven't you given him the chance to explain, and why run away?"

"Don't you think it's bizarre that we've been friends all this time and not once did he let on he wasn't just plain ordinary Doug?"

"Did he ever say he was plain ordinary Doug?"

"Well no... I just assumed he was run-of-the-mill," said Cheryl.

"So how is it his fault, if you assumed something about him?" questioned Laura.

"Put like that...okay, but what about him being filthy rich?"

"What about it?" countered her sister. "Did he lie and say he was on the breadline, standing in line at the food banks?"

"Of course not, but he didn't say he wasn't and that's just as bad."

"Tell me, Cheryl, how does someone tell another person that they are loaded?"

"I don't know, you tell me, you've got all the answers." said an increasingly cross Cheryl.

"Hey, I've not got all the answers, but c'mon. What would you expect him to say? By the way, my dear, I'm a billionaire. Is that okay?"

"You're being ridiculous. Of course he should have told me he was rich. I have been prattling on about being skint and not having enough to pay the rent, or my credit card bill, and all the while he's doing multi-million pound deals."

"Get real. Did he ever offer to help you out financially?" asked Laura.

"All the time, but of course I wouldn't accept his help. It was just general moaning, you know what I mean. God, he must have thought I was a complete dork."

"I think he probably thought he'd met someone who for once wasn't after what they could screw out of him."

"Well, there's no chance of that happening now. And all the gifts are winging their way back to him as we speak."

"What? You sent it all back? The ring and everything, you didn't just hold on to a little keepsake? Maybe just twenty five or even thirty thousand, for old times' sake?"

"No, I didn't. Now you know it all, please let it go. I really don't want to go over and over it."

"Okay," said her sister, "we'll see. Goodnight."

Doug

Fat friends turn a see-saw into a catapult.

For the first time in God knows how many years, Douglas Winthrop III was at a loss. He paced about his New York apartment, had cancelled all his scheduled meetings and not picked up on his emails for days. All because of a woman. Not just any woman, he truly thought she was 'the one'. Smart, sassy or feisty, as the Brits called it, and she had unceremoniously dumped him, and by text – how low was that?

He had to hand it to her; she certainly played the long game. Stringing him along, making him believe they were two of a kind – she had called them soulmates and he had believed her. Okay, so they lived different lives, but that wasn't a problem. He'd offered to help her out financially several times, but she'd always declined, which he'd admired and respected. She was her own woman. He was sure that would change when they got married, or so he had thought, but the ring must have proved to be a step too far.

Mark, his assistant, and also his best friend, had taken a call from Van Cleef concerning the ring. Apparently they had been contacted by some London jeweller looking for a valuation and because it had been a specially commissioned piece, they had been alerted.

Doug should have told her it was insured, and put her mind at rest, but with everything that was going on, it had slipped his mind. Well, she had a nice little haul. If she'd waited a bit longer she could have skinned him for much more. He had never intended to have a pre-nuptial agreement, even though she'd always insisted they must. They'd jokingly had the conversation many times, with Cheryl always insisting he wasn't getting his hands on her twenty year old banger and a pre-nuptial was a must. Like most Brits she hated talking money and always seemed a bit embarrassed about the subject. Maybe she didn't talk about it, but she could sure deal with it. Ironically, his lawyers were working on the terms now and he had just signed off the first draft. Wow, had he had a near miss?

Mark was concerned by Doug's behaviour. The guy was a workaholic and here he was, head of one of the US Fortune 500 corporations, mooning around his office like a lovesick teenager. It was five days since he had received the Dear John text and Mark couldn't for the life of him understand what Doug was all about. He needed to snap out of this and get back on the ball. Doug swam in a shark-infested sea, and the sharks were circling.

The parcel had lain on his desk for a couple of days when, through sheer boredom, Doug got round to opening it. What the hell was all this? Pulling out strands of pearls, a Tiffany necklace, a couple of watches and the Van Cleef & Arpels ring box. It took a few moments for him to register what he was holding. All the gifts he given her over the past year were here. What did that mean, he asked himself? Why had she sent everything back? Well, she sure as hell wasn't a golddigger. She wasn't after him for his money. Truthfully, he had never believed she was, but what other explanation could there have been?

It was straight to voicemail for the umpteenth time and no reply to his emails. Time to go another route, he thought. Loath as he was to mix business with pleasure, he had no choice. He had to get to the bottom of this. Armed with what little information he had, he placed a call to the CEO of Unicorp Ltd.

"Who's the top IT guy we have on the payroll?" he buzzed through to Mark.

"It depends on what you want, there are a couple."

"I need to trace someone and I may have left it too late. They would need to access personal emails and voicemails and it has to be discreet, no blabbing. They will also be well paid."

"Do you want them to work from here or at the office?"

"Here, and fast, I've left this long enough."

Two scruffy individuals arrived within the hour and set to work. By early afternoon they had a log of every call Cheryl had made along with copies of her emails, sent and received. They had also hacked into CCTV showing Cheryl arriving in Marbella, meeting up with a small blonde person, presumably her sister, and heading off in a white PunTo: registration B33457 MAL.

Following the car along the main highway from the airport to Marbella, they had lost them. They managed to pick the car up again, parked in La Calle Escuelas, where it remained all night.

E-mail from cheryl.mason@unicorp.com to info@unicorp.humanresources
Subject: Leave of Absence
I am sorry to give such short notice, however, I have been called away to deal with a family crisis. I am prepared to take this as unpaid leave and once again apologise for such short notice.
Cheryl Mason
Tech Support.

-oOo-

E-mail from cheryl.mason@unicorp.com to selena.buckingham@unicorp.com
Subject: Running away.
Don't be mad at me, but I couldn't deal with the situation. It's much better if I do it this way. I have sent all the treasure back. Hope I still have a job when I get back. Keep up with the diet.
Love Cheryl.
Explain to the others.

-oOo-

E-mail from cheryl.mason@unicorp.com to
laura.mason21@hofmail.esp
Subject: Running away.
Hi Sis,

Got a bed for a couple of weeks? Life is awful
and I need to get away. I'm booked on Ryanair 10:50
to Malaga tomorrow, arriving at 12:50, meet me at
Arrivals. If not, I'll get a cab.

Luv big sis xx

-o0o-

E-mail from laura.mason21@hofmail.esp
to: cheryl.mason@unicorp.com
Surely you're not a runaway bride this soon?
Of course you can have a bed.
I will be outside the airport waiting.
Luv
Little sis.

-o0o-

E-mail to info@ryanair/ticket
Subject: Boarding Pass Flight Number RYN 3450
please print.............................

-o0o-

JULIE

Keep your friends close and your enemies fat.

It was a couple of days before Julie realised Cheryl had not been at work. Was she ill? Had something else on the fiancé-front happened? She hoped Cheryl and that Selena hadn't gone behind her back and got supplies of the new wonder drug, after all, it was her discovery. She might just stop by and check in on Selena later in the morning.

It was still taking her much longer to do her rounds than it used to. She was still the main source of information on Chunky Monkey a.k.a. The Reluctant Bride. Oh, yes, she had managed to let that little gem slip and the Fish Girl, what was it she was called? Colossal Kylie. Most of the girls in the building had something to ask about their progress and to be fair, many of them were genuinely interested. But, there were a few that were not so genuine and we all know from experience the harm and despair that a few can cause.

She'd been quite disappointed in the reaction from Cheryl and Selena. They didn't seem to realise what a monumental discovery they were on the brink of. Didn't they realise it would change dieting for ever? Just imagine being able to eat anything and as much of it as you liked and still remain slim. It was incredible, in fact, it was almost impossible to believe, but she had seen it with her own eyes. She just had to get to Douglas Winthrop III. So near and yet so far.

Apparently Cheryl had taken leave of absence. In Julie's mind it was leave of her senses. What in heaven's name had made her go gallivanting off to get over heartbreak? God, with the money and lifestyle she would enjoy being Mrs Douglas Winthrop III she could pay someone to suffer for her. Hadn't she, Julie, got over a really messy divorce? Wasn't Selena struggling with the fact she might never have children? So really, Cheryl was being a teensy weensy bit self-indulgent.

Was that Sir Ronald, heading for Human Resources? How unusual, in fact unheard of. He never ventured down from the top floor. Julie didn't think he'd ever stepped out of the elevator on any other floor bar the top. Well, she'd just trot along behind him; he wouldn't know she was off the beaten path.

The girls in Human Resources were all of a flutter. He wanted details on a particular employee and it was top secret. So top secret he couldn't even tell them. Well, that was going to be a problem, because he couldn't access the system, and without the name they couldn't help him. What a farce.

"Excuse me, Sir Ronald," piped up Julie. "Maybe I can be of service?"

"And you are?" boomed the slightly flustered CEO.

"Julie, sir. I'm Julie from the post room."

"And...?"

"Well, I believe you have something of a delicate request is that right?" Julie asked nervously.

"Mmm."

"Well, why don't I access the information?"

"And why would you be more confidential than these people here?"

"I told you, I'm from the post room. Julie's my name, you might have heard of me? Everyone knows that the post room knows everything first."

"Makes sense. Go on, clear off, the rest of you. Okay, Julie-from-the-post-room, this is the information I need."

"Oh, I don't need to access her file, sir. I can tell you exactly where she is and what she's doing."

Thank goodness she had managed to catch Selena at lunch time.

Kylie

I'm not overweight – just 9" too short.

Nibbling on another biscuit, she surfed the net for miracle diets. She found more pills, potions and patches, all promising spectacular results and next day delivery.

If one pill taken three times a day lost ten pounds, then surely two pills would lose twenty? This, together with a patch to stave off hunger and a shake to replace meals, was a no-brainer. She'd be in the dress by Friday, or sooner.

So on a breakfast of three pills, two patches and the peculiar-looking shake, Kylie strolled the hundred yards from her house to the bus stop. Cheerfully reasoning that there was no need for extensive exercise regimes as the miracle programmes would do the work for her.

She clocked in with seconds to spare, and was that a disappointed Bill she spied scurrying away? This was getting ridiculous; she was definitely going to get one of her brothers to have a word. Or maybe Jason should? However, the little time they had spent together the last few weeks was worrying. She never seemed to be on the same time zone as him. He was either working overtime, or visiting his mates, none of whom she knew, but they all knew Mandy, or his latest was washing his hair. She wasn't overly concerned, because when he saw her in the dress it would be worth everything.

Popping another couple of pills and swigging a mouthful of the mustard coloured shake to carry her through till lunch, Kylie worked like she'd never worked before. In fact, the handlers couldn't keep up with her and were complaining bitterly, having had such an easy ride with her before.

She's on drugs, they complained, she has to be on drugs, she's never done this much work in a week, never mind a morning. The boys in packing were equally astounded. They too couldn't keep up with her. "Hmmm, no more stupid jokes from them," she chuckled and, feeling the pangs of hunger setting in, she blithely popped a couple more pills and finished the shake, which by now tasted fabulous. She could actually feel the fat melting away. Jesus, she might even lose the first ten pounds today.

Lunch time came and went without a break, she just kept on working. Everyone was talking about her. So what. It just went to prove what she'd always known. She was good, she was very good. And to tell her that, along came Bill who looked decidedly smug. She was to accompany him to Mr Thomkins in Human Resources. God, what had she done now? They couldn't complain she wasn't up to the job, she'd proved that tenfold today. She had not been late for the past three weeks and had never clocked off early.

So what could they blame her for now? Of course, it wasn't something wrong, she had completed her probationary period. Going by her work today they might even make her a supervisor. By heavens, there were a few who would live to regret the day they had crossed her. First to go would be Poofy Pete, who was still complaining about his silly little paper cut. Kylie the supervisor – how good did that sound?

CHERYL

Can fat people go skinny dipping?

True to her word, Laura hadn't bombarded her sister with questions concerning her love life, or lack of it. She knew Cheryl would open up in her own good time. And she was right. It took till day three for her to mention Doug's name and by day five Laura knew most of what had gone on and why Cheryl had acted the way she had.

The sisters, though close, were completely different in temperament. Cheryl was a knee-jerk person. Whatever situation or circumstance she found herself to be in, she reacted immediately and not always with the best results; this case being a perfect illustration. But just as she was a knee-jerker, she would never accept help or advice from anyone, including her sister. She always had to deal with problems herself. Laura had learned over the years that the trick with Cheryl was to let her come to the right conclusion by herself, with just the merest of nudges.

A week had gone by in a flash; the sisters had spent the days lying on the beach soaking up the warm Spanish sun and in the evenings soaking up copious amounts of warm Spanish plonk.

Despite her heartache, Cheryl had loved being with her sister and resolved to spend more time with her, whatever happened in the future. The break was exactly what the doctor had ordered. Cheryl was okay, not good nor bad, just okay, but she missed Doug more than she would have believed possible. She came to the conclusion that she wasn't going to feel any better or worse staying away from home.

It was time to face reality. She had heard from both Selena and Julie a couple of times. Selena was extremely concerned for her friend and pleaded with her to return to work as soon as possible as 'things were going on'.

Julie's messages on the other hand, were as usual, all about Julie. Apparently she'd had some bizarre encounter with the chairman of the company and now she alone had his confidence.

Cheryl had come to a decision, she was going home and back to work. She might as well face the music and start looking for another job. Laura was so disappointed. She had loved being with her big sister and she was so proud of the new Cheryl. This stunning, golden, tanned being was a far cry from the frumpish, self-effacing, withdrawn woman she'd left six months ago. Whatever Doug's reasons and motives had been, he had certainly been a good influence in one respect.

On their last night together the girls ventured out into the nightlife of Marbella. Millionaire's playground, and for the first time ever in her life, Cheryl didn't look, or more importantly, feel out of place. Okay, she was wearing second-hand Spanish charity shop stock.

None of her old wardrobe fitted her! She looked fabulous and the two girls were attracting more than their fair share of admirers as they wandered along the marina in Puerto Banās, the place to be seen. A place only a few months ago Cheryl would have avoided like the plague. Oh! My! God!

Doug

He couldn't fathom what had made Cheryl change her mind, but he wouldn't rest or get closure until he found out. He knew she wasn't after his money, it just wasn't an issue. In the past it was the dollar signs that his so-called girlfriends were attracted to, not him. Hey, as soon as the money went, so did they. But with Cheryl, wealth didn't come into it and he thought she had liked him for who, not what, he was. Doug was definitely sure that there was no-one else, so what could it be? Fifty thousand feet above the Atlantic, he played every scenario over in his mind. Was she sick? Was she married? Did she have ten kids? (Oh God, he hoped not!) What had happened?

The pilot announced they were ten minutes from landing, so hopefully he would soon have the answer. The plan was to go straight to the yacht from the airstrip; no need to broadcast his arrival, everything in Douglas Winthrop III's world was kept on standby.

He and his small entourage would be well taken care of on board the luxury cruiser and far more discreetly than in any of the five star hotels lining the marina.

It was some time since he'd been in Marbella and it had been one of the places on his honeymoon list.

After a sumptuous dinner Doug, Mark and Patti, Mark's current girlfriend, wandered aimlessly around the harbour area, taking in the sights and on the lookout for their quarry. Marbella was not an easy place to hide, despite the crowds of beautiful people. Everyone congregated on the main thoroughfare so it was fairly easy to spot a missing bride.

They would begin their search in earnest tomorrow, but tonight, caught between jet lag and exhaustion, it was a leisurely stroll and early to bed.

Twice Mark thought he'd caught a glimpse of Cheryl, but he had no intention of drawing Doug's attention to the girl. In fact he'd brought Patti along on the trip mainly as a distraction for Doug. Hoping that by the time they did actually catch up with Cheryl, the billionaire would be firmly enamoured with a new beau. A couple of day's holiday would do him nicely and tomorrow was another day.

Still on New York time, Doug was up and on deck at daybreak. The marina and the surrounding streets were empty, apart from a few late night / early morning revellers and with the crew not due to be on duty for an hour or so, he had time to do a little exploring on his own. Donning his running kit, off he set. He knew the general direction of Laura's apartment so he saw no harm in scouting round.

As he approached her apartment block there were obvious signs of life; he saw two women packing a car and he was pretty sure it was his fiancé and her sister. Were they going on another journey? Should he make himself known? Doug didn't have to make that decision; it was taken out of his hands, as he'd been spotted by Laura.

"Well, well, it seems we have an early visitor, sis. What's wrong? Did your girlfriend kick you out of bed?" Laura sneered.

"What?" Doug answered. "What girlfriend? Out of bed where? I was under the impression that this person here was my girlfriend, sorry soulmate, fiancée, whatever. And I certainly didn't get the opportunity to kick anyone out of bed. Hey, Cheryl, nothing to say to me? Not even hello?"

"What's to say? You made a fool out of me and it's over. Now, if you'll excuse me, I've got a flight to catch."

"You're going nowhere," Doug persisted. "Not until I get to the bottom of this mess. What am I supposed to have done? Just how did I make a fool of you? I went off on a business trip, leaving you happy and pleased we were going to be married and I come back to a TEXT, a damned text, saying we're through. Hey girl, a bit low wouldn't you say after all this time? Why? And can we please move out of the street?"

"No, we can't, I've got to be at the airport in twenty minutes, so no. Go back to your girlfriend and leave me alone."

"What girlfriend? Who are you talking about?" the Texan drawled. "You're the only girl I've spoken to in the last couple of years, so I have no idea where this is coming from."

"The woman you were with last night. The small blonde. I'm sure even with your selective memory you could remember her."

"The small blonde is Mark's girl. She's nothing to do with me, he brought her along. And that still doesn't explain the text."

"I saw you both last night, arm-in-arm, staring into each other's eyes."

"WHAT? We were arm-in-arm to stay together, all of Spain was out last night, and as for staring into her eyes, God knows."

"Really? I'm not interested, I have to go, I'll miss my flight. Let's go, Laura." Cheryl got into the car.

"Forget your flight, I'll fly you back. You are not going anywhere until we sort this."

"See, you think because you're rich you can order me about. You think you can buy me with all your money. Pretending to be ordinary just like us, it's sick and no, you can't fly me back. I'd rather go myself."

"Can I ask you something?" said Laura from the sidelines. "Why are you in Marbella, and when did you plan this trip? Cheryl, listen to what he has to say..."

"Look, before I start on any heart-wrenching story, can I please have some coffee and get off the sidewalk?"

Reluctantly, Cheryl stood aside while Laura and the big Texan, her future brother-in-law, made their way back into the apartment.

Armed with his coffee, Doug answered Laura's questions.

"I knew it," Laura challenged her sister. "I knew you'd got the wrong end of the stick. So Doug travelled thousands of miles to find you and you still can't see it."

"He's rich!" shouted Cheryl.

"So bloody what," her sister replied. "If he wasn't, he wouldn't have been able to find you, stupid mare."

"C'mon Doug, show me this fabulous cruiser and if she's too stubborn to come with us, you can marry me, I'm a much better catch," laughed the younger girl.

CHERYL

Dear Santa, this year please give a me big fat bank account and a slim body.
Please don't mix those two up like you did last year

OMG. It couldn't be him, but it was and it certainly hadn't taken him long to get over his broken heart. There he was, strolling arm in arm with a beautiful young woman, staring lovingly into each other's eyes. Well, no way was he going to see her in her hand-me-down clothes, only one step up from a beach bum. Grabbing Laura by the arm, she pulled the unsuspecting girl into a crowded bar, ordering her to get some drinks.

Dodging behind the crowds she watched Doug and his new woman wandering through the melée.

Laura came back, fighting her way through the throng with their drinks. Cheryl immediately set them down and hauled her sister onto the next, equally busy, terrace bar full of beautiful people.

"Hey, do you know how much drinks cost in these places? You've been hanging out with rich folks too long," she laughed.

"Same again," Cheryl ordered Laura.

"Forget it. Just what are you up to? Have you seen someone? Don't tell me you've seen someone you want to cop off with?" She laughed. "Well, if you're going to get another billionaire this is the place to find one."

"Shut up and follow me." Cheryl was keeping Doug and his new woman just in sight. They had been joined by a young guy and she watched the little party turn down the gangway and board a fabulous cruiser.

"I would have said out of our league, but not in your case," giggled her sister. "That's probably their dinghy."

"Funneee! Okay let's go" snapped Cheryl. "There's nothing more to see here."

"Sorry! Did I miss something? Do you know these people?"

"Well, I know one of them and he didn't take long to get a replacement me."

"Eh, who's replacing you? I'm lost. OMG, do you mean to tell me that's him?"

"Yes, but what on earth is he doing here? Whatever it is, it's nothing to do with me."

"Maybe he came to find you."

"I don't think so. Anyway, nobody knows where I am, and did he bring her along as a spare?"

"Well, we'll soon find out," said her sister who was already halfway along the boardwalk.

Laura was all set for a confrontation.

"Come back, you idiot" said Cheryl. "Do you honestly think I would want him back after that little demonstration? I think I've had a lucky escape."

"I'm loath to agree with you, but maybe you did.

Mind you, he must have thought a lot of you at one time."

"How do you make that out?" said Cheryl.

"Look at the name on the side."

"Cheryl 1. He probably changes the name with every conquest. I bet if we come back tomorrow it'll be Natalie 1 or Olivia 1. I wouldn't attach too much importance to that."

"Let's go, I've got an early start tomorrow. Thank God I decided to go back, imagine bumping into him with his new concubine. My God, I'd just die of embarrassment."

The girls walked the short distance back to Laura's apartment in silence, both deep in their own thoughts.

Selena

What you are good at? Let's see,
I'm good at cooking. I'm good at eating.

This was going to be quite a week for Selena – tomorrow they would all find out about their jobs. This was, of course, an unofficial statement, but damned near as good as one. Julie had been privy to what was going on and in an effort to stem the hysteria rising throughout the company, the chairman's confidante had taken it on herself to impart the news. She comforted those who were going to have to look elsewhere and celebrated with those who were safe. This was much better than a cold and unemotional interview with HR she told herself.

All large companies should have a Julie, or so Julie thought. She knew what redundancy packages were on offer and made sure everyone had the information to allow for some bargaining power. She herself was one of the not-so-fortunate, although the post room per se was remaining. Somehow she was expendable. That was not how Julie conveyed the message to her colleagues. Her version was all about cutbacks and finances and time to give a youngster a chance at far less cost. Everyone knew it was rubbish, but so what, she had more than served her purpose.

The second issue and the most important one, as

far as Selena was concerned, was her meeting with the IVF team. She had battled continuously and conscientiously with her weight. She'd never missed a week of her slimming club, unlike the others and whilst she had tried lots of different diets she had done the absolute best she could. She knew it would be touch and go, and she fervently hoped they would give her a bit of leeway.

She had a few weeks between the interview and the start of the programme. Selena had one last throw of the dice, she had heard of a new treatment which could take inches off everywhere and a bit of weight, but it was extremely expensive and not always guaranteed. It was also very much about timing so she had booked herself an appointment at 9am on the day of her interview. This would give her six hours where she hoped to take off at least ten pounds. She could but try.

It transpired that her employment status would almost remain the same. A small raise in her salary, otherwise no great change.

She had been for the controversial treatment at 9am. After being wrapped in yards and yards of cling film and basically being shoved in an oven, this treatment was guaranteed to lose inches and pounds. Selena thought she was going to die. The heat was unbearable but she had to persevere.

Fantastically, she had lost almost 8lbs and ten inches off her boobs, chest and hips. The clothes she had been wearing on arrival literally hung on her. Now she had to get home and change for the most important interview of her life.

There were four panellists, all very pleasant, who did their level best to allay her fears. There were a number of tests and, as usual, dozens of forms to be filled out and Selena was sent off with her dedicated nurse to jump through various hoops. First thing on the agenda was height and weight. She tried standing on one leg; caught. One foot on the floor; caught. Eventually she just had to stand on the scales properly.

"Tut, tut," said her dedicated nurse.

"Is there something wrong?" asked Selena.

"No no, just would have liked a bit more off," said the nurse.

"Well, I've tried my absolute best, I couldn't do any more."

"Don't worry, my dear."

And so the afternoon went on. Eventually it was back to the panel.

Selena had known from the minute she entered the room that the answer was a no and she had great difficulty in concentrating on what was being said. Test results and blood pressure and weight and God alone knew what else. Then the dreaded words; I am sorry. Selena couldn't take any more; she just wanted to get out of the room.

OMG. She seemed to be expanding right before their very eyes. Her clothes were getting tighter and tighter and then there was a ripping sound. The shrinking treatment was wearing off and poor Selena looked like a huge black pudding ready to shed its skin. She was mortified!

"Look, I did my best and if you'd give me a few more weeks I'll get down to the required weight."

"Again, I am sorry..."

"No you're not," she interrupted, muttering to herself. "I will, I can lose another ten pounds, I promise."

"I am sorry, yet again..."

"Don't say you're sorry when you bloody well couldn't care less," she said under her breath.

"There would be no possibility of you losing more weight and we certainly wouldn't recommend it, not in your condition."

The words 'your condition' pierced her thought process.

"What condition?" whispered Selena.

"Mrs Buckingham, I am delighted to inform you that you do not qualify for this treatment because you are already pregnant."

Fried chicken, rice and peas were definitely on the menu tonight, after all she was eating for two!

JULIE

This was to be her last post round in the building. She knew it would take forever, but so what? Everyone would want to wish her well and there were bound to be little gifts, tokens of their esteem, and of course, this would be a great chance to network for her new venture. Everyone knew about her new venture. In fact most of her colleagues were sick to death of her new venture.

The main party for those leaving was being held on Saturday and of course Julie would be attending, after all it wouldn't be a party if she wasn't there, the most popular employee in the company. It really was such a shame she was leaving and few employees could understand why? Or so they said, but today was for her unofficial goodbyes. She had a supply of tissues and had worn heavy-duty waterproof mascara, no tears.

It had taken her some time to get through to Douglas Winthrop III, but with her usual tenacity she had at last tracked him down to his cruiser, sailing with the future Mrs Winthrop III. It certainly hadn't take him long to replace what's-her-name.

Cheryl (that's it) had just disappeared one day. Probably sold all that lovely jewellery and bought herself a little cottage somewhere and now kept six cats. It failed to penetrate Julie's thick skull that it was only just a couple of months since they had all joined Fat Fighters and that this was highly unlikely. Although if she knew the real story she'd be the one having kittens.

First floor. "Morning girls, now I don't want a fuss and I certainly don't want any tears," she quipped as she distributed the mail.

"Em, tears?" ventured one girl.

"Yes, tears. Today is my last day. From now on Julie will be no more," she said, beaming expectantly at them all.

"Oh, good luck Julie."

"Yes, see you around."

"We must meet up for lunch."

Well, she thought, that was a bit flat. Never mind, Sales next and they were amongst her favourites.

As it turned out the entire sales force was ensconced in the boardroom going over the projected sales for the coming year.

IT Support on the fourth floor. Not a soul looked up from their screens, not even when she knocked over the water cooler (never on purpose, surely?) As it turned out, Julie completed her very last post round in record time and since there was really nothing else for her to do, she got what was unheard of in the company, an early bath.

Saturday would be different; they would all say their goodbyes then. It was too emotional face to face. And of course she would meet Douglas Winthrop

III, her benefactor. Having tracked him down and bombarded him with emails and voicemails, he had reluctantly conceded to her proposal. The details would be finalised soon. She was so determined and had such conviction, she was prepared to sink her life savings into the venture and wouldn't be dissuaded otherwise. Although Doug knew the product was a real breakthrough in weight management, he wasn't convinced it was the money making scheme Julie thought it was.

He had endeavoured to talk her out of it but no, she was convinced it was a winner.

DOUG, CHERYL & JULIE

Cheryl had never known life could be so...she didn't have the words to describe how things had changed. Mainly thanks to her younger sister. If Laura hadn't taken the bull by the horns, the twosome would probably still be arguing in the middle of a Spanish street. If ever two people had been at cross-purposes it was these two. Cheryl's argument that she had not known of her fiancé's wealth still stood.

However, on Doug's part, he firmly believed that she had known and was completely au fait with it. They had had many in depth conversations in the past about the failure of his first venture and how he had risen to the top again through hard work and perseverance, so when he'd sent her gifts from Tiffany's, he had presumed she would know their value. He found it hilarious that a Hermès bag, which he had beaten Michelle Obama to and had cost somewhere in the region of $50K, Cheryl had thought cost $40 from a flea market.

"OMG, I'll never use it again," squealed Cheryl.

"That's okay 'cos I've already snaffled it," her sister joked, waving the fabulous bag under Cheryl's nose.

Doug was worried. He was worried that things would change, that she wouldn't be able to cope with the vast differences in their lifestyles. But he hadn't counted on the tenacity of a younger sister.

Cheryl and Laura had always been endearingly close and more so since their parents had passed away. Their mother had died when Cheryl was ten and Laura seven and they had been in the care of various aunts because their father worked abroad. They had had a happy enough childhood, but formed a tight little pod of them and their father. When he was killed in a freak accident, the girls were in their teens and it drew them even closer. There was no way Laura was going to allow anything to stop her sister's happiness with this man.

So he was rich. Good, she thought, she's never going to have to worry if she can pay the grocery bill.

So he had a private jet. Good, she thought, no queuing in the baggage hall for hours.

So he had a luxury cruiser. Good, she thought, she'd only ever been on the Isle of Wight ferry.

So he had homes all over the world. Good, she thought, plenty of room for her to stay without getting under their feet.

No, she wasn't letting this one slip away, no matter how stubborn her big sis could be. She had to keep them together for as long as possible, just to seal the deal.

With a bit of gentle persuasion Laura talked her sister into staying on board and having a few stress-free days.

"Let's face it," she told Cheryl. "We probably won't get a chance like this again, not if you're still determined to dump the poor guy."

So they had spent a week of unadulterated fun and excitement aboard the Cheryl 1. Each day the cruiser left the marina and took off for somewhere exotic. The other passengers made a pact to leave the young couple alone as much as possible.

Cheryl and Doug swam and sunbathed in deserted coves. They followed a pod of dolphins, wandered round the old city of Marrakesh, taking in the wonderful smells and sounds of the ancient souk. Ate fabulous food in little known places and finally made love under velvety, starlit skies.

"If I die tomorrow, I'll die a happy man," whispered Doug.

"Me too," replied Cheryl. "No, I don't mean I'll die a man," she laughed. "It's just that I never knew I could be so happy."

"So, are you still going to marry me?" He teased.

"If you'll still have me." replied his fiancée coyly.

Doug shot out of bed and, hastily pulling on his shorts, dived out of the cabin, leaving Cheryl somewhat bemused.

"I'll take that as a no," she muttered. "Oh, well, it was nice while it lasted" and determined not to show her despair, she went off to find her sister. It was time to head back to reality.

She saw very little of Doug the next day, or anyone else for that matter, they all seemed to be very preoccupied and she was being left to her own devices. Good, freedom to make her getaway plans; they would leave when the others went to dress for dinner. She didn't want to face some protracted farewell. She'd had a fabulous time and she loved him dearly, but no way was she overstaying her welcome. Time to pack, well that wouldn't take long, she smiled.

Back in the stateroom, laid out on the bed was the most magnificent cream lace gown, satin shoes and a beautiful delicate posy of cream roses and bride's breath. What was going on? Was it fancy dress? If it was, it was a bit over the top.

A knock on the door interrupted her thoughts and standing there was her sister, in the most stunning turquoise gown.

"C'mon girl, get a wiggle on. It's not every day I get to be bridesmaid at my sister's wedding."

"Wedding? Whose wedding?"

"Yours, you silly muppet. I officially gave my permission this morning and you are about to become Mrs Douglas Winthrop III."

"But how?" Cheryl questioned.

"The Captain," answered her smart sister. "Doug and I thought why wait? Mind you, I wouldn't want to do this again, so no divorce."

The cruiser had been decorated from bow to stern with arches and garlands of cream roses. There was a magnificent array of food and drinks and approximately thirty guests, including her three not-so-fat friends.

Both Doug and Laura had been in touch with the threesome and it hadn't taken much persuasion to have them fly over to celebrate the wedding. Let's face it, who would turn down the opportunity of a private jet and five star accommodation?

Julie, grinning like the cat that had got the cream, was waving what looked to be some kind of contract at her. Lord, had she actually persuaded Doug? Well, it looked like she had got her heart's desire.

Selena was glowing, pregnancy obviously suited her. Imagine all that torture and deprivation, only to discover she'd been pregnant all the while. There was no doubt she too had her heart's desire.

Last but not least there was Kylie, who had, as she put it, 'failed miserably at the diet lark' but who looked fabulous. She'd got in tow with Madam Jessica and formed a joint venture to create a plus size designer range. Whoever said that clothes maketh the man, or in this case, girl, was dead right.

Kylie was unrecognisable as the lass from the fish factory; she looked like something straight out of the pages of Hello! magazine.

It had been a wonderful evening and the wedding guests had partied well into the wee small hours, no-one wanted it to end. Naturally, the last guests to leave were her slimming buddies. She promised to keep in touch but she knew the reality was 'slim'. She did, however, have a question for one of them.

"Julie, before you go, can I ask you about your new venture?"

"Of course," she said dancing over to the bride.

"How old exactly is your dog?"

"My dog? Cheryl, I've not got a dog. Why would you think that?"

"Oh, nothing, never mind. I've obviously got the wrong end of the stick. Good luck and remember to keep in touch."

Julie had every intention of keeping in touch, she was sure Doug would want to keep an entrepreneur of her calibre close to his chest.

"Did you tell her?" Cheryl asked Doug back in their stateroom.

"I tried, honestly I tried and I did my best to put her off," answered the groom.

"So she still doesn't realise that it's a veterinary product?"

"No, I don't think so. She could always call it Fat Fighters FUR U."

They collapsed laughing.

Printed in Great Britain
by Amazon

49544817R00095